It was sex. Pure and simple.

That's what this was. Nothing more. Nothing less.

Linc knocked on Regina's door and she opened it immediately. The dampness of the ends of her curls and her change of clothes told him she'd taken a quick shower. The look in her eyes told him she'd been looking forward to this moment as much as he had.

She wore a simple pair of jeans that were anything but simple on her curvy frame, and a plain pink T-shirt that was anything but plain.

Damn, but she was beautiful.

And sexier than any woman had a right to be.

He cleared his throat. "Hi."

She smiled. "Hi."

And then he was kissing her.

Linc wasn't clear on how he moved from Point A to Point B so quickly. All he knew was that one moment he was closing her apartment door... the next he was pretty near swallowing her whole.

And she was eagerly returning his hungry attentions.

It seemed both of them were intent on making sure she didn't fall asleep again....

Blaze

Dear Reader,

What happens when the subject of your investigation becomes the object of your desire? We've used the "stakeout" theme before, but never quite in this red-hot way....

In *Wicked Pleasures,* tall, dark and dangerous Lazarus Security partner Lincoln Williams is only interested in one thing—his job. It's not until sexy Regina Dodson catches him with his pants and guard down that he starts to question the imbalance in his life. But what happens when Regina discovers the true reason behind Linc's interest in her?

We hope Linc and Regina's soul-searing story keeps you awake long past your bedtime...and tempts you to pick up the third and final title in the Pleasure Seekers series, *Undeniable Pleasures,* featuring Jason Savage (from *Reckless Pleasures*) next month.

We'd love to hear what you think. Contact us at P.O. Box 12271, Toledo, OH 43612, or visit us on the web at www.toricarrington.net or www.facebook.com/toricarrington, where there's fun to be had every day.

Here's wishing you love, romance and HOT reading.

Lori & Tony Karayianni
aka Tori Carrington

P.S. Check out the Blaze Authors' Pet Project at www.blazeauthors.com.

Tori Carrington

WICKED PLEASURES

TORONTO NEW YORK LONDON
AMSTERDAM PARIS SYDNEY HAMBURG
STOCKHOLM ATHENS TOKYO MILAN MADRID
PRAGUE WARSAW BUDAPEST AUCKLAND

Recycling programs
for this product may
not exist in your area.

ISBN-13: 978-0-373-79627-4

WICKED PLEASURES

Copyright © 2011 by Lori Karayianni & Tony Karayianni

ABOUT THE AUTHOR

RT Book Reviews Career Achievement Award-winning, bestselling duo Lori and Tony Karayianni are the power behind the pen name Tori Carrington. Their over fifty novels to date include numerous Harlequin Blaze miniseries, as well as the ongoing Sofie Metropolis, P.I. comedic mystery series with another publisher. Visit www.toricarrington.net and www.sofiemetro.com for more information on the couple and their titles.

Books by Tori Carrington

HARLEQUIN BLAZE

To get the inside scoop on Harlequin Blaze and its talented writers, be sure to check out blazeauthors.com.

Don't miss any of our special offers. Write to us at the following address for information on our newest releases.

Harlequin Reader Service
U.S.: 3010 Walden Ave., P.O. Box 1325, Buffalo, NY 14269
Canadian: P.O. Box 609, Fort Erie, Ont. L2A 5X3

We dedicate this story to miniseries-loving readers everywhere; life is about connection, so why shouldn't that also apply to the books we read and write? And, as always, to editor extraordinaire Brenda Chin, who puts the "it" into editor...

_1_

LINCOLN WILLIAMS knew two things to be true: he was damn good at his job…and he was damn good at his job.

The rest…well, the rest was a crapshoot.

As the only son of a single Caucasian mother and an African-American father he had never met, he'd been relegated to the fence separating each culture: not white enough to feel completely comfortable in his mother's world; not dark enough to belong in the unfamiliar black community.

So he'd learned early on that the only thing he could control were his actions. And it was those actions on which he insisted he be judged. Not by verbal agreement, but by tacit understanding. It wasn't until he'd become first a Marine, then was recruited into the FBI at Quantico, that he'd come into his own. Learned not only to embrace his preference to go unnoticed, but to use it to his advantage. Something he was damn good at, despite his height of six foot four and muscular two-hundred-and-fifty-pound build.

Of course, only he knew about his recurring dream of disappearing altogether.

It was on the heels of just such a nightmare that he'd abruptly resigned his position with the Bureau ten months ago and signed on with fellow ex-Marines to establish Lazarus Security based in Colorado Springs, Colorado. Their most public success to date was assisting in the recovery of a missing seven-year-old girl in Florida.

But what Linc had to do now was in no way connected to Lazarus: a man he had helped put away for a thirty-year term of incarceration had just escaped. And he fully intended to return him to the six-by-eight-foot cell where he belonged.

If his reasons stretched beyond the fact that he'd been the one to capture the sadistic criminal two years ago while still with the Bureau…well, that was between him and his target.

Thankfully, the Friday staff meeting at Lazarus didn't include anything that required his undivided attention.

He looked over the twenty recruits listening to two of the partners, Megan McGowan and Darius Folsom, as they went over ongoing assignments and upcoming contracts. Just before they drew the meeting to a close, Linc ducked out of the room, as was his M.O. at every meeting.

"Hey." Dari caught up with him afterward. "You good with contacting your sources on the James contact?"

"Check."

His longtime friend, fellow Marine and now business partner grinned. "Didn't have to ask, did I?"

Linc glanced at him.

"Hey, why don't you drop by the Barracks later? We're putting together details on Jason's surprise birthday party next week."

"I'll see what I can do."

The Barracks was a bar and Linc was known to stop in from time to time, mostly to appease his friends who liked to unwind at the local establishment. He had other plans tonight, but figured it shouldn't take too long to toss a few bucks into the kitty for a gift for their fellow partner. Especially since it wasn't that long ago that Dari and Megan—who were as much partners outside Lazarus as inside—nearly split because of something that went down with Jason.

It was reassuring to see things were back on track.

Besides, soon Dari would be reclassified as combat ready, following an injury he suffered a month ago, and redeployed overseas. He'd like to spend a little time with him before that happened.

Dari smacked a hand against his shoulder and said, "Hope to see you there."

They parted ways, Linc heading for a room designated as his office, although it was a space he spent very little time in. He had everything he needed on him, which was the way he preferred to work. But this afternoon he wanted to wrap up a few business-related items so he'd be free to pursue his personal agenda.

Namely, to apprehend one Billy "the Bank Robber" Johnson and return his ass to jail where he belonged.

And he knew exactly where to start: with Johnson's girlfriend, Regina Dodson.

"Come on, Regina! You act like you're sixty instead of twenty-six. I finally talked you into coming out with me. Is it too much to ask you to actually have fun?"

Regina Dodson thought it was more than an act; she felt sixty. And had for a good long time. Too long. It was one of the reasons she'd reluctantly agreed to come out with Vivienne tonight. The outgoing redhead was the first friend she'd made when she moved from Livermore Falls, Maine, to Colorado Springs a year and a half ago.

Moved? More like escaped. She'd packed up everything, changed her name and was making a new life for herself in the small city nestled against the Rocky Mountains south of Denver.

Still, there wasn't a day when she didn't wake up terrified this would be the day her past would catch up with her.

And for some odd reason, lately she couldn't help feeling she was being watched.

She absently rubbed her arm and then took in Vivienne's animated face over the rim of the margarita she'd been nursing for a good two hours. Club lights blinked, dance music pulsed and all she could think about was how much she wanted to go home and climb into bed with a good book. Funnily enough, it was through books she and her friend had originally met; more specifically, a library book club to which they both belonged. They were the only two unmarried women in the group that didn't have kids, and were under the age of a hundred, as her friend liked to say.

"You need a drink," Vivienne pronounced, waving for the bartender.

Regina held up her margarita. "I have a drink."

"No, you need one you can't pretend to sip for hours on end." The girl stepped in front of them. "Six shots of tequila. And don't forget the salt and lemon."

Regina stared at her. "I'm not drinking six shots of tequila."

"You're right, you're not." The woman behind the bar lined up six shot glasses and began filling them. "You're going to drink three," Vivienne added.

"I'm not drinking any," Regina said over the sound of the loud music, scanning the throng around them. Too many people.

She'd never been much of a drinker. One glass of wine with dinner every now and again was about as adventurous as she got.

Vivienne paid the bill and then edged one of the shot glasses in Regina's direction. She licked the back of her hand between index finger and thumb and then sprinkled salt there before pulling a bowl of sliced lemons closer, nodding for her to do the same.

"Ready?"

"Viv…"

"Come on. What's the worst that can happen? The ice wall around you might melt?"

Regina drew her head back. "There's no ice wall around me."

"No? I've watched you freeze out four great-looking guys in an hour. What would *you* call it?"

"Smart?"

All four had reminded her of her ex in some way: the first in looks; the second in attitude; the third in his approach; and finally the fourth in his choice of clothing.

Of course, Santa Claus would probably remind her of her ex at this point.

Over recent months, Vivienne had ceaselessly invited her out and she'd ceaselessly resisted. It had only been in the past few weeks she'd finally stopped reading every word of every online newspaper searching for signs that shadows from the past were about to stretch over and suffocate her present.

Still…she wasn't quite ready to go out and act like a carefree single woman just yet.

Viv laughed and nudged her shot glass even closer. "One. You can at least do that for me."

Regina stretched her neck. "One?"

Her friend smiled.

If that's what it was going to take to shut Viv up, Regina figured she could handle that.

So why did she have a feeling those were going to be her famous last words?

She followed Viv's lead, licked her hand and then sprinkled salt on it. On the count of three, they simultaneously licked the salt, downed the shots of tequila and then quickly took a lemon slice and sucked on it.

Viv hooted. Regina shuddered.

"Another!"

She should have known her friend wouldn't settle for stopping there. But rather than be upset, she found herself laughing. The seemingly harmless liquid was already beginning to warm her insides, as if it were, indeed, melting the ice wall to which Viv referred.

She shook salt onto the back of her hand and reached

for the second shot. Viv cheered and counted to three. They both smacked the shot glasses onto the bar and then reached for the lemon.

Before she knew what she was doing, she was downing the third shot.

Regina smiled. She had to admit, the liquor was beginning to soften the world's hard edges. She leaned against the bar rather than standing ramrod straight. Thankfully, every guy no longer seemed a variation on her ex. The lights looked soothing instead of garish. The music wended around and around her, making her want to dance. Something she hadn't done in a long, long, long time.

Something she'd never expected to do again.

Vivienne raised her hand to wave the bartender back, but Regina caught her arm. "No more."

Her smile must have convinced her friend that she had, indeed, been cured, because Viv laughed and grabbed Regina's hand instead.

"Let's dance."

Suddenly, it seemed like the best idea she'd heard all night…

TEN STOOLS DOWN, Linc watched the scene between the two women. He'd have known Willa Nelson aka Regina Dodson anywhere, despite the lengths she'd gone to to change her appearance along with her name. Where once her hair had been wheat blond, long and straight, now it was a warm honey brown and curly, barely brushing her slender shoulders.

At one time he might have needed to physically trail someone in order to track their activities, but now he had but to plug their cell-phone number into a high-tech app in his own cell phone and their location popped up. When he'd seen Regina was at a downtown club, he'd immediately gone there, wondering if Johnson might try to contact her.

When he'd gotten word a couple of days ago on Johnson's escape, and he'd looked up Willa's whereabouts, he'd been surprised to find she'd moved into his own backyard. Of course, he hadn't lived in Colorado two years ago—"home" had been little more than a standard-issue Bureau box of an apartment in D.C. then. But to discover they both lived in the same place seemed like more than coincidence; it appeared providential.

From his safe, invisible position down the bar, he'd watched Regina's friend—he knew her name was Vivienne Cruise—coax his target into doing tequila shots. He'd been slightly amused at Regina's open shudder at the first…and surprised, then intrigued when she'd gone on to do the second and third.

The two women were now dancing. And he suspected that even if he didn't have to watch Regina, he would have anyway. There was something ultimately alluring about the hesitant yet intrinsically sexy way she moved her slender body, despite the shapeless green dress and low heels she wore, contrasting with her friend's fire-engine-red skirt and blouse and strappy black stilettos.

An odd couple if ever there was one.

The friend caught his gaze from across the room.

Damn.

He turned back toward the bar, but caught sight of the woman in the mirror as she grabbed Regina's hand and started in his direction…

2

"WHERE ARE we going?" Regina asked, nearly stumbling trying to keep up with Vivienne's long strides toward a destination she couldn't see. Still, you weren't supposed to fight the hand leading you. And she was feeling good. Perhaps a little too good.

"Well, hello there."

Regina realized they had stopped. She stepped up next to her friend to find her addressing the wide back of a guy seated at the bar.

At first Regina thought he wasn't going to respond. Then he slowly turned, looking her full in the face.

She caught her breath.

"My God!" Vivienne said. "You look just like that wrestler…or actor. What's his name? The Rock."

Regina fairly gulped as she stared into the man's pitch-black eyes. While she understood the comparison her friend was making, this guy was different in significant ways from the actor. First of all, his features weren't as sharp, but more angular. Second, he was slimmer, his build more ropy than bulky.

She took in his simple black T-shirt and dark denim

jeans and then blinked to look back up into his mesmerizing eyes. He had yet to acknowledge her friend.

"Hi," Viv said, obviously amused. "My name's Vivienne. And the one you're interested in is Regina. What's your name?"

"Lincoln."

Vivienne's smile widened. "Wanna dance, Linc?"

His brows rose as he looked them over. "With both of you?"

"Uh-huh," Viv confirmed.

Regina glanced at her. She wanted all three of them to dance together? She raised a hand to her forehead, pushing her hair back, wondering if it had been a good idea to drink those shots…

"Sure."

Before she knew what was happening, she was back on the dance floor between Viv and Linc. She hadn't realized he was so tall when he was sitting on the stool, but now he towered over her by a good foot. Her friend put her hands on her hips from behind and swiveled her to stand face-to-face with Linc. She stumbled and he automatically reached to balance her.

"I've always wanted to do that dance from my favorite movie!" Vivienne said from behind her.

"What movie?" Regina asked.

"*Dirty Dancing.* You know, the one where Jennifer Grey dances with Patrick Swayze and his partner?" She reached for her right hand and then Linc's and put them together, then resumed her place behind Regina, complete with hands on her hips.

Regina slowly looked up into Linc's striking face. God, but he was handsome. And the way he looked at her melted away whatever might be left of her reserve. Her heart thudded loudly in her ears, nearly drowning out the music. Her skin tingled all over. And an ache she hadn't experienced in what seemed like forever took up residence between her thighs.

"Come on," Vivienne said. "Let's move."

Linc moved his right foot forward and she dropped her left one back as Vivienne did the same behind her, the hands on her hips guiding her into the next step.

There was something naughtily hot about the movement. Especially when Linc leaned in closer, points of his body making contact with hers. Mmm...he smelled good. Like deep woods and fresh air and hot male. And his hand where it held hers was big and warm, sending little shocks of sensation up her arms and across her chest, hardening her nipples under her dress.

Much, much too much time had passed since she'd been this close to a man. Her senses didn't seem to know what to do with the overwhelming input washing over them. Of course, the alcohol probably heightened that effect.

Just then, Regina didn't care how or why she'd come to be in that particular spot at that particular time. She was merely enjoying that she was. And didn't want to be anywhere else...

DAMN, SHE WAS INTOXICATING.

Linc wasn't much of a drinker—he preferred to remain in control at all times—but on the few occasions he had indulged, he'd had a similar rush to the one he was feeling right now, looking down into Regina's face.

He easily led the steps Vivienne suggested, finding the scene reenactment subtly sexy. The movie was one of his aunt's favorites and he'd been forced to watch it with her no fewer than a dozen times over the years during his visits.

Somehow in all his research, he'd missed the fact that Regina was stunningly attractive. Then again, maybe he hadn't missed it so much as hadn't anticipated his reaction to her being this close. It wasn't often he came into face-to-face contact with one of his subjects, much less cheek to cheek.

His gaze skimmed her features, taking in the arch of her soft brows, the sizzling warmth in her green eyes, the almost poutlike quirk of her full lips. This close up he also understood that she wasn't as thin as he'd originally thought. There wasn't a single sharp angle to her.

His jeans tightened incrementally with each brush of his body against hers.

She readjusted her hand in his. He looked at her fingers and short, clean nails, totally unlike the bloodred polished ones her friend had. He knew Regina worked as a waitress at a small downtown diner and imagined she must do a lot to keep her hands as soft as they were.

He'd already guessed she didn't drink often. If he needed further proof of that, her unsteadiness on her feet was clear evidence.

As she swayed toward him, his body instantly reacted, need, sure and swift, exploding through him.

"Sorry." He saw her speak the word rather than

hear it as she looked up into his face, her nose mere millimeters from his.

He swallowed hard, wanting to kiss her so much in that one moment it was all he could do to stop himself.

Interestingly, he didn't have to. Because she kissed him.

He wasn't surprised to find she tasted as good as she looked. Strawberry lip gloss teased his taste buds even as the tang of tequila remained on her breath.

"I say we get out of here," Vivienne said behind her.

Regina blinked and drew away. "What?"

"I don't think the lady's ready to leave yet," Linc said, not wanting to let her go just then.

"I meant the three of us…"

Linc looked from Regina to Vivienne and back again.

He couldn't have agreed more…

3

REGINA TRIED TO open her eyes, but she feared they were fused shut. She rubbed her eyelids and then blinked against the bright morning sunlight flooding the bedroom in her small apartment. Her head pounded and her body ached in places she hadn't been consciously aware of until that very moment. She groaned and closed her eyes again, rolling over…straight into something.

Before totally registering someone else was in the bed, she was out of it. It took her a moment to realize she wore nothing but her birthday suit. She grabbed the throw that had been lying on top of her bed but was now on the floor.

A groan and then the figure under the sheet rolled over.

"Vivienne!" she said. "For God's sake, you scared me half to death."

"Why are you whispering?" Her friend smiled and looked around. "Is this your bed?"

Regina pulled the throw closer. Sleepovers had never been part of the plan before. Never mind open nakedness. Viv's casual tone inched her uneasiness higher.

Slowly but surely, some of last night's even~~ts~~ out in her mind. Little more than blurry snippets of candlelight, music, wine and more, um, dirty dancing in the living room.

And her and Linc and other naughty goings-on.

Oh, no…

She stared at the bed, her heart hammering in her throat even as heat warmed her blood.

"What happened?" Viv asked, stripping back the top sheet.

Regina started to close her eyes to keep from seeing more than she wanted, then realized her friend was wearing her bra and underpants—red satin with black lace. The type of lingerie Regina would never dare buy herself no matter how much she might want to.

She let out a long breath. While the undergarments weren't what she was used to seeing her friend in, it wasn't complete nudity. She'd seen more of her in her bathing suit.

"Coffee?"

Regina squealed at the sound of the male voice behind her. She whirled to face none other than the guy they'd met at the bar last night.

He was here?

Still?

Her gaze trailed to the bed, to him and back.

Oh, no…

His grin was one hundred percent pure sin.

"Sorry. Didn't mean to startle you."

His words contradicted his naughty expression.

He openly looked her over, his gaze lingering in

...rywhere but on her
...on her face.

...she held the throw between her
...em both bare. When she'd faced him,
...d twisted around her legs, her pubis clearly
...

She gasped and turned around to adjust the material, then realized she was giving him a full back view. She couldn't move fast enough to cover herself even as she ducked into the connecting bathroom.

Oh, no…oh, no…oh, no…

Regina leaned against the doorjamb, her eyes closed, her lungs refusing air.

This wasn't happening… It wasn't even remotely possible she…

What was going on?

Her mind reeled, racing from one thought to the next. Had all three of them spent the night together? In the apartment? In her bed?

She remembered kissing Linc. She ran her tongue over her lower lip. Boy, did she ever remember kissing Linc. And she even recalled some clothing removal. And soft moans. And…

Oh, God…

INCREDIBLE. She was even more beautiful in the morning. Short hair mussed and framing her face. Smudged mascara darkening her eyes, her mouth swollen.

Linc put down the coffee cups on the nightstand, noticing the way Vivienne lay back in the bed staring at him invitingly.

An invitation he wasn't interested in acknowledging much less accepting.

"Well," she said with a suggestive purr. "Since Reggie couldn't tell me what happened last night, perhaps you can."

He smiled rather than grimaced. "I'm heading out. Pass on my goodbyes."

"Leaving so soon?" she asked. "Don't hurry out on account of me."

She was exactly the reason he was leaving.

"Nice meeting you, um…both," he said.

Within moments, he was closing the front door of the ground-level apartment behind him. It would be nice if he could leave the image of Regina's nakedness behind as easily.

Oh, nothing had happened. At least nothing near what the two women might believe. Not because the opportunity hadn't existed. But in the end, no matter how attracted he'd been to Regina, he hadn't been able to take advantage of her when she'd been so obviously intoxicated.

The memory of the taste of her mouth made him groan even as he allowed himself the freedom to recall exactly what had gone down last night. And what hadn't…

They'd returned to the small apartment complex on the edge of town, a place like many that was short on quality but high on location, the view of the Rocky Mountains to the west enough to make a hole-ridden tent look appealing. He'd viewed it from the outside on several occasions over the past few days, but it was the first time he'd gotten a glimpse inside. He'd been surprised to find it so stark, barren of all sign of the woman who lived there. Well, except for the stacks of books, some that bore the plastic covers indicating they came from the library.

It reminded him of his place.

As he climbed into his company SUV, he ousted the reflection and replaced it with the memory of kissing Regina.

Or had she been kissing him?

Definitely a mutual kiss.

They'd been dancing in her living room, her face alluring in the flicker of the candlelight. Her friend Vivienne had essentially passed out on the sofa, an empty bottle of Merlot tucked in her arm, leaving him alone for all intents and purposes with Regina. Which is what he'd been angling for all evening.

She'd seemed to read his thoughts and swayed into him, her mouth millimeters from his.

Oh, he'd kissed her all right.

And kissed her and kissed her and kissed her.

He couldn't recall a time when he'd enjoyed feeling a woman's mouth against his so much.

Then she'd pressed her hips against his in an instinctively female way that set his every male instinct ablaze and he'd suddenly wanted much, much more.

In that one moment, he hadn't cared if she stumbled a bit when he walked her toward her bedroom. He'd only known an intense desire to be buried deep inside her. To watch her mouth open in a soft moan. To hear her throaty sounds as they had sex.

They were no sooner in the bedroom than she was pulling open his jeans while simultaneously trying to strip him of his T-shirt. He'd chuckled, helping her even as she tugged at her own clothes.

Within seconds they were both naked…and she was dropping to her knees to take his pulsing length into her sweet mouth.

Linc swallowed hard, his jeans tightening at the mere memory. It had felt so good having her attention focused so intensely on pleasing him. More, it appeared she drew pleasure from the sexual act. He knew plenty of women who did it as part of a show, looking up at him perhaps in approval, or to check to make sure they were getting the reaction they were after. Not Regina. Her attention was solely on what she was doing.

And oh, she had done it so very, very well…

He hadn't planned to come, but he couldn't help himself. She'd easily adjusted, smoothing his semen over his still-hard length then licking him clean.

Hell, he'd nearly come again just watching her.

Then she'd stood up and nearly fell over.

And he knew he couldn't take it any further.

He groaned now as he had then. He'd had every expectation that sex with her would be even better than the blow job, but he'd known it wasn't a good idea to go any further than they had. Especially since he was afraid he'd allowed things to go too far already. He didn't want her regretting anything that passed between the two of them. Ever.

As he drove toward his own apartment across town, he reminded himself there was another, primary reason why he needed to keep her friendly: she was the key to his catching her ex.

He grimaced. How had a woman like Regina ever

become involved with the likes of Billy Johnson? It was a thought he wouldn't have entertained for more than two moments before. Who cared, so long as he met his objective? But now that he'd spent a little time with her, he couldn't help wondering what she'd found attractive in the no-good criminal.

As far as he could tell, she led a clean life. Even under her own name, she held no record.

She was the only child of a single mother. She'd grown up and had lived her entire life in the small town of Livermore Falls, Maine…until leaving after Johnson's sentencing.

Could limited options have been the reason she'd hooked up with Johnson? A check of an online high school yearbook found Johnson had graduated two years before her. In a town where the entire senior class was only thirty students, he figured opportunities would have been greatly limited.

It was something with which he personally couldn't identify having grown up in the Bronx, where he couldn't have named ten percent of his graduating class much less every one of them.

At any rate, that was a long time ago.

His cell rang. He picked up on the second ring. "Yeah."

"Some information came in on that fugitive."

One of his contacts from Quantico.

"Shoot."

"There's a report out of August, Maine. It's believed he was pulled over for speeding eighteen hours ago."

"They're holding him?"

"No, they let him go. They didn't realize who they had until an hour afterward."

Linc had heard far too many stories of a similar nature. Close calls, near misses. Of course, in this case, it was probably a good idea the officer hadn't been following national news bulletins or he might have ended up dead.

He didn't see Billy Johnson allowing himself to get nabbed during a routine traffic stop. Had the officer tried to arrest him, no doubt Johnson would have pulled out the gun he undoubtedly had. And he would have used it.

"So he's hanging around home, then."

"Looks that way."

He thanked the contact and disconnected even as he pulled into the parking lot of his apartment complex. Ten minutes. That's all it would take for him to grab a shower, dress and be back out in the car. He needed to check in at Lazarus, then map out Johnson's possible whereabouts and try to figure out where he might be heading next.

And how long it would take him to make his way to Colorado Springs.

In the meantime, it was still a good idea to stick as close to Regina as possible.

His immediate jolt of desire at the prospect made him grimace…

4

"HEY! WATCH IT!"

Regina grabbed napkins from the table holder to mop up the water she'd just accidentally spilled on a guest. "I'm so sorry. I don't know where my head is today."

A lie, to be sure. She knew exactly where her head was. And where it had been all morning.

She was an hour into the lunch rush and this was the second time she'd spilled something. Unfortunately, the first time had been coffee. Fortunately, it hadn't been on the customer.

Seeing as she worked mostly for tips, she figured she could rule out getting anything from the upset businessman who snatched the napkins from her and then waved her away.

Sigh.

She hadn't been scheduled to work until later that afternoon, but the owner, Trudy Grant, had asked her to come in when one of the other waitresses called in sick. No matter how much she would have liked to decline, she could use the extra money. And anyway, she'd hoped keeping busy would take her mind off other, um, uncomfortable thoughts.

When she'd finally come out of the bathroom earlier that morning, she'd found Linc gone and Viv dressed. She and her friend sat down in the kitchen to drink the coffee he'd brought them (if that's what you could call her choking down a small portion of it), but she'd quickly found out Viv wasn't any more enlightened on the previous evening's events than she was.

"God, I hope nothing happened," Viv had said.

Regina had nodded in full agreement, relieved she shared her hope.

"Although not for the same reason as you, I suspect." She'd sipped her coffee loudly. "If something like that goes down, I want to remember every last sweet moment of it."

Regina had found an excuse to usher her friend and her outlandish ideas out of the apartment as quickly as possible. Then she'd spent the next two hours frenetically cleaning the place from top to bottom, although it hadn't needed it. The physical activity had made her feel marginally better. But when she'd gone in to catch a shower, she'd discovered her mind going straight back to Linc and the night before.

She distinctly remembered him backing her into her bedroom…kissing…lots of kissing…and then she'd gotten down on her knees…and…

Oh, hell…

She spilled water from the pitcher again, this time on her way back to the kitchen. Brian, the busboy, shook his head and grabbed a mop to clean it up before someone slipped on the wet tile.

"Are you all right?" Trudy asked.

Regina finally put the water pitcher down and wiped her damp palms on the front of her white apron. "Late, um, night."

"You? Well, then, you must tell me all about it."

LINC SPOTTED REGINA the instant he walked into the diner.

It was just after seven and the dinner crowd was mostly gone. Regina sat at the end of the counter. One of her shoes was off and she slowly rubbed her bare foot against the shin of her other leg, engrossed in something she was reading in front of her. She was half turned away from the door, so he could see little more than her profile. But even in her plain gray uniform and white apron, her hair pulled up haphazardly, she was still the prettiest girl in the room, regardless of what room or how empty or full it was.

Damn. He'd hoped seeing her again would provide the evidence he needed to prove she was nothing special; allow him to forget how incredible it felt to have her full mouth on him. Instead, he couldn't help noticing what made her unique, and the desire to sample that mouth seemed to have doubled.

Regina lifted her head as if hearing something. Then she turned and met his gaze as if knowing he was there looking at her.

He couldn't help smiling.

And his groin tightened when she easily smiled back.

"Can I help you?" a girl who was probably no older than sixteen asked.

"I've got it, Tiffany," Regina said, coming up behind her.

"I thought you clocked out?"

"Well, I just clocked back in."

"Whatever." The girl walked off.

Linc chuckled and Regina smiled.

"Need I ask if this is a coincidence?" she said, motioning for him to take a seat at one of the front booths. He slid in and she did the same opposite him.

"Is what a coincidence?"

"This. Your stopping by the same diner where I work."

His grin widened. "You suggested I stop by. Remember?"

She looked down at her hands in her lap.

"You don't…"

Of course she didn't, he knew. She hadn't said one word about where she worked. But he guessed she recalled very little about last night, which left him a lot of room in which to wiggle. And he planned on doing a lot of moving. Whatever it took to nab her ex.

His objective tonight was to find out if she'd heard from Billy. And if she had, to get an idea of where he might be.

"Did I suggest anything specific?" she asked. "You know, did I invite you here or…?"

He squinted at her, trying to follow her line of thinking. Then he shook his head. "No. I'm just here for a meal. And some good company."

She pulled one of the menus in a stand free and slid it in front of him. She looked ill at ease. Much like this morning. Only with clothes.

He found his gaze dropping to where the material of her uniform stretched against her chest. Not overly generous, but he'd seen enough the night before to leave him with a lasting impression. Along with a lingering desire to sample each.

"Look," she said, clearly uncomfortable. "Before you order, I need to ask you something…"

He waited, not about to let her off the hook she strained against, but not enjoying watching her struggle nonetheless.

The truth remained that he could have easily taken advantage of her last night. And while he got the distinct impression she'd been acting out of character and wasn't the type to indulge in one-night stands with perfect strangers, well, what could he say he knew about her?

And what if it had been someone else her friend had pulled up to dance?

"Okay, I don't know how to say this except just to say it," she said finally. She lifted her eyes to stare into his. "Did we…sleep together last night?"

He liked her directness. As well as the earnest expression on her face. As if prepared to face the consequences, whatever they may be.

"You don't remember anything?" He was a little disappointed she didn't remember putting her mouth on him. Especially considering the impact it'd had on him.

Her lashes created shadows on her cheeks as she looked down, a pink blush covering her skin. But if he wasn't mistaken, there was a little, naughty quirk to her lips as she said, "Well, I remember one thing…"

Linc shifted in the booth. So she did recall their encounter. That pleased him.

"Nothing happened," he said.

She blinked to look at him. "Pardon me?"

His gaze locked with hers and for a moment, everything seemed to stop.

He wasn't sure what it was about this one woman, but she seemed capable of seeing him in a way he hadn't been seen in a good long time. And it both calmed and agitated him.

"Well," he said quietly, sure his own lips were doing a bit of quirking. "Outside the one, um, thing…"

She laughed.

The sound was a welcome and sexy surprise. It told him she wasn't sorry about what had passed between them, while leaving the door open for perhaps something more. Still, it spoke of her relief that her memory wasn't faulty.

"Nothing?" she asked, a decidedly suggestive glint emerging in her green eyes.

His pants grew tighter. "Yet."

"So are you going to sit here with him or wait on him?"

Linc hadn't heard the irritating teen waitress approach until she popped her gum and intruded on the moment with her question.

He watched Regina's smile widen as she reached down to take off her apron and fold it on the table in front of her. "I'm hungry. How about you?" she asked him.

Suddenly he was ravenous. And not for anything on the menu, either…

THE NIGHT WAS PLEASANT enough compared to the recent heat wave they'd been experiencing lately, and the air was filled with the scent of flowers. So much unlike summers in Maine when evenings like these might require a sweater.

Regina couldn't remember a time when she'd so thoroughly enjoyed a man's company doing something as simple as taking a walk after a meal.

"Haven't you been on your feet all day?" Linc asked.

They both looked down at her sensible, thick-soled shoes, reminding her she still wore her uniform. Funny, she half expected to be clad in something comfortably appealing, based on how she felt.

"Yes."

"Would you prefer to go someplace where we can sit?"

She shook her head. "No. I'm actually enjoying a walk longer than the length of the diner. Besides, this is nice."

Silence fell between them, something it seemed to do often. Linc didn't appear to be a man much for talk. And she liked that about him. Liked that there could be quiet without either of them feeling the need to fill it.

And for the first time in what seemed like forever, she felt...safe somehow. As if she didn't have to keep looking over her shoulder, waiting for the shadow dogging her heels to rise up and suffocate her.

"So, are you from Colorado Springs?" she asked.

"No. New York."

"City or State?"

"Technically, both."

"I can't say as I've ever met anyone actually from New York City."

"Well, you can now."

He had a great smile. One that seemed to surprise him as much as it did her whenever he used it.

"Which part?" she asked.

He hesitated for a heartbeat. Something that might go unnoticed in mixed company, but that she made a mental note of. "The Bronx."

"I'm from Maine," she offered without being asked, surprising herself. The story she'd concocted to protect herself had her from Boise. Why had she just told him the truth?

"I thought you said you were from Idaho?"

"Did I?" She must have shared more than she realized last night. What else had she said? She hoped not too much. She'd been so good over the past year and a half. So why was she revealing so much about herself now? And why to him?

"Yes."

She tried for a casual laugh. "I must have been really drunk."

"And you told me you were from Idaho because you were afraid I'd look you up?"

"Something like that." She moved closer to him as another couple approached from the opposite direction. Her arm brushed his, sending shivers across her skin. "So, you know I work at a diner…"

"And are studying, if the books I saw you poring over earlier are any indication."

She'd stowed the textbooks in her car before they

went for their walk. "Yes, I'm studying to become a registered nurse. I volunteer ten hours a week at Beth El."

He didn't look surprised.

"So what do you do?"

"Me?"

"Mmm."

"What do you think I do?"

"If I had to guess..." She looked over his close-fitting T-shirt and jeans with an appreciative eye. "Personal trainer?"

His chuckle filled the night. "A personal trainer?"

"Yes. Why is that amusing?"

"So, I look dense?"

"What, are you saying personal trainers are stupid?"

He didn't respond, merely shook his head and continued walking.

"So what *do* you do then?"

"I'm in security."

She was a little more careful with her response this time. "Like a night watchman?"

His chuckle tickled her ear. "Slightly more advanced."

"Oh?"

His answer was another smile.

"Okay. A mystery."

"Hopefully one you don't feel compelled to solve."

"Don't worry. I'm not going to do an internet search on you." His expression sharpened. "I'm not that kind of girl."

A heartbeat of silence and then he offered, "Maybe you should be."

His words struck her as odd, and her footsteps slowed until she'd stopped altogether.

5

OKAY, ON the moron-o-meter, that comment ranked somewhere between asinine and flat-out stupid.

"I'm just saying that in this day and age, well, checking someone out may not be a bad idea. The technology's there—it's dumb not to take advantage of it."

"Is that what you do? Do you perform background checks?"

"No."

She'd resumed walking and he slowed his steps to allow her to catch up.

"I'm a partner in a private security firm. We handle various aspects of a company's needs."

"And before that?"

"I was a Marine."

He kept his eyes trained forward but felt her gaze on his profile for a long moment.

"I can see that," she said quietly.

He looked at her.

"My father was a Marine," she said.

He hadn't known that. Of course, her background

material merely noted the basics: father deceased when she was six.

"Once a Marine, always a Marine," he said.

The light briefly left her eyes. "Yes, well, then my dad is a Marine with wings. He was killed in combat when I was young."

"I'm sorry."

"Thanks." She looked down at her feet and then at him. "What about your dad?"

He shrugged.

"Would you rather not talk about it?"

"There's really nothing to talk about. I don't know my father outside the name on my birth certificate."

A long silence and then she asked, "Have you thought of looking for him?"

"Why?"

"I don't know. Closure, I suppose."

"I'm not even sure he knows he has a son."

"Don't you think he deserves to know?"

"What?" He stared at her.

"I guess I worded that wrong—wouldn't you want to know if you had a son out there?"

He'd never quite looked at it that way before.

The truth was, his mother had never really mentioned his father outside of saying he wouldn't want to have anything to do with him. He had been a one-night stand. And both his parents had been no more than sixteen at the time. Linc had been raised by his aunt.

He hadn't realized he'd spoken the words out loud until Regina asked, "What happened to your mom?"

Lord. Had he ever told anyone this before? He must have at some point. But damned if he could remember.

Which made it doubly interesting that he was sharing the information so easily with Regina.

"She moved to L.A. when I was an infant. I barely saw her while I was growing up. I talk to her every now and again, but for all intents and purposes, my aunt has always been my maternal figure."

Her arm brushed against his and then she was entwining her fingers with his. He was glad for the touch and squeezed her hand. The desire to squeeze much, much more was growing with every step they took.

"My mom and I were always close," she said quietly. "I miss her now we're so far apart."

"She still in Maine?"

She nodded and then looked in the opposite direction as if to keep him from seeing her expression. "I keep trying to talk her into moving out here with me, but… well, she says that's where she was born, that's where they'll bury her."

She looked sad somehow. Alone.

And Linc was surprised by the desire to protect her that surged within him.

Before he knew that's what he had in mind, he was tugging her close and tilting her chin up so he could look directly into her face. Her mouth hung open slightly, both in surprise and, he guessed, anticipation.

He kissed her.

REGINA'S EVERY MUSCLE melted like a marshmallow over a fire. Funny, Linc seemed to taste exactly like that. Somewhere in the recesses of her mind, she understood that it was because he'd had a piece of Trudy's chocolate-marshmallow pie. But right then, she couldn't seem to concentrate on anything beyond the way her heart pounded an uneven rhythm in her chest, and how her mouth watered with the desire for Linc to deepen the kiss.

Then he did…

His tongue stroked hers in a slow, deliberate way that robbed her of breath and made her tighten her hands where they rested on the hard muscles of his upper arms. He leaned into her and she discovered, with a silent moan, that his arms weren't the only hard thing she was able to feel.

The memory of having taken his long, thick length into her mouth the night before might have made her blush…but not now. Right now, all that was on her mind was the desire to enjoy tasting him without the blurriness of drink.

"Damn," he said quietly as he broke off the kiss but made no move to resume walking.

"What?" she whispered.

He looked into her eyes and the impact was just as powerful as his kiss had been.

"I never thought I'd hear myself say these words. Your place or mine?"

Her throat was so thick she nearly couldn't speak. "Which is closest?" she managed to whisper.

"Yours."

"Then mine it is…"

LINC HAD BEEN THINKING about this moment ever since forcing himself to push Regina away the night before. And it was proving sweeter than he could have imagined.

Twenty minutes after their kiss on the sidewalk, they stood in her bedroom, a small lamp from the living room casting a soft, red glow against her skin where she stood naked in front of him. The moment they closed the front door, they'd come together like a couple of thirsty travelers, kissing and tearing at each other's clothes as they stumbled their way to the bedroom.

And now here they both stood, about to fulfill what had begun the instant their gazes met at the club last night.

Regina's fingers skimmed around the girth of his erection and then firmly grasped him. The air hissed from his mouth at her confident touch. She moved her hand, causing his hips to buck involuntarily.

He wanted to be inside her. Now...

He drew her closer, kissing her deeply, reveling in the feel of her taut nipples against his chest, her hand trapped between them. He skimmed his fingers down her back and over her firm bottom, then sought out her shallow channel from behind. He groaned without sound. So wet...so ready...

"Protection," she rasped.

He continued kissing her. "What?"

"Condom. Do you have one?"

God, she tasted like ripe fruit. "No. Don't you?"

She made a low sound and then stepped back, leaving him practically panting in front of her.

"Oh, hell. You've got to be kidding me." He ran his hands over the top of his close-cropped hair several times in barely concealed agitation.

This wasn't happening. Not twice in as many nights. If he were a superstitious man, he might think the Fates were trying to tell him something. But he wasn't and even if they were, he had no intention of listening.

"There doesn't happen to be a drugstore that delivers, would there?"

Her laugh released a bit of his pent-up need. "Nope. Although that's a good idea. Think of the business they'd get."

Damn. Damn, damn, damn, damn.

He reached for his jeans that were near the bedroom door. Leaving her standing there, looking so ready to be made love to, had to be the most difficult thing he'd done in a good long while.

"Where's the closest place?"

"About a mile up the road."

"Of course. It couldn't be up the block, could it?"

She reached for her clothes.

He caught her hand. "Don't."

She blinked at him.

He scooped her up and deposited her on top of her bed. God, but she looked so incredibly sexy, her honey-brown hair tousled around her face, her mouth swollen from his kisses, her breasts full and accessible. It was all he could do not to beg her to go without protection just this once.

"Don't move a muscle," he said.

Her laugh was almost gigglelike, touching something inside him.

He couldn't have moved any faster for the door had he broken into a run.

REGINA LAY BACK against her bed, listening as the door slammed closed behind Linc. She smiled and snuggled deeper into the bedding, squeezing her thighs tightly together, delighting in the tiny shivers that swept over her skin.

She felt giddy and high and feverish, and none of it had a thing to do with alcohol. She skimmed her hands over her hypersensitive breasts, catching her breath at her immediate response to her own touch. Her nipples were so hard and achy. She swallowed, edging her right hand down her trembling abdomen. She spread her thighs slightly and slid her fingers into the damp tangle of curls there. She stretched her neck, realizing she could come so easily...

She slowly drew her index finger the length of her shallow crevice, unable to remember the last time she'd been so wet and needy. Correction, unwilling to. All she wanted to think about was the here and now. And Linc...

She recalled their interaction last night in bits and pieces, but nothing had prepared her for holding his length in her palm tonight. So long, so big...

She groaned as the tip of her finger dipped into the pool of heat between her legs. Her heartbeat quickened and just like that she achieved orgasm...

6

LINC WAS SWEATIER when he finally returned to Regina's apartment than after his morning ten-mile run when the air temperature was at least twenty degrees hotter. He let himself into her apartment, tearing into the box of condoms he'd just purchased as he strode toward her bedroom. He should probably climb into the shower first, but...

The hell with a shower.

He stopped in her bedroom door. She was right where he'd left her. Beautiful, bare...and fast asleep.

For the second time that night, he let out a string of curses.

This was not happening...

He stood in the doorway for a long moment, taking in the way her hand rested on her upper thigh, the curve of her breasts, the sound of her soft snores.

He knew she'd been on the job since early that morning. He also knew she hadn't gotten much sleep the night before. And, of course, worry over what had or had not happened had probably worn her out on top of the physical stress.

He thought about catching that shower and then climbing into bed next to her, rousing her from sleep. But considering they barely knew each other, he decided that wouldn't be much better than taking advantage of her while she was intoxicated.

Damn. Damn, damn, damn, damn.

He quietly put the half-opened box of condoms on her nightstand and then reached to push a soft curl from her brow before covering her with the top sheet. She was so out of it, she didn't move a muscle.

Moments later he stood outside her door, battling back the urge to go back inside. He thought of a handful of phone numbers he could call, but no matter how much he wanted release, he only wanted it with the woman sleeping in the apartment behind him.

Another run, maybe. Yes. And a nice, long, cold shower…

Two DAYS LATER, Regina tightened her boxing gloves and then gave the punching bag another one-two whack. Over the past year and a half, she'd taken nearly every self-defense class available. Then, at the health club she'd joined, she'd stumbled across boxing classes. The physical activity made her feel better somehow. One of the pros suggested it was like aiming darts at a picture of someone unlikable…but better. She agreed.

Especially now.

She still couldn't believe it had happened again. She'd woken Sunday morning to find herself pretty much in the same position Linc had left her, a box of condoms on the nightstand along with a note: "Didn't want to wake you." He'd signed it simply "L" and included his phone number.

She'd beat the pillow down and then gone to the gym to do a better job on a punching bag.

She couldn't even allow herself to entertain the idea of calling the number he'd left so she might apologize.

At this point, she wouldn't be surprised if he never wanted to see her again.

She lost focus and the bag swung and hit her in the shoulder, nearly knocking her off balance.

"You're supposed to hit it, I think, not the other way around," Vivienne said from the doorway of a connecting room filled with other fitness equipment where the majority of club members worked out.

Regina caught the bag and then wiped the sweat from her brow with her bare forearm. "Every now and again I like to let it think it stands a chance."

"Speaking of hitting things, you ready to hit the showers?"

She sighed. "Yeah."

Thankfully, Vivienne hadn't mentioned Friday night again, both of them back into the regular workweek swing of things. Viv was a paralegal at a midsize law firm, and Regina had attended classes in the morning, then worked the lunch shift at the diner. They met three times a week at the club, depending on their schedules.

She'd debated telling her friend about Linc's visit to the diner Saturday night, then decided against it. There was no sense saying anything if she was pretty sure she wasn't going to see him again.

She grimaced as they walked to the showers. Besides,

she didn't want to chance her friend's asking to be included in any future goings-on.

"Oh, he's new," Viv said, openly appreciating a guy lifting weights as they passed.

Regina gave an eye roll as she untied her right glove with her teeth and then pulled it free. "You're impossible."

"No, I'm single." She put her arm over Regina's shoulder. "And so are you. Now, where are we going to eat afterward…?"

"HEY, EVERYTHING ALL RIGHT?"

Linc stared at where Jason Savage stepped in front of the crosshairs of his semiautomatic rifle, blocking the target. He swung the weapon so it pointed toward the dirt of the Lazarus training grounds.

"Shit, Savage. I could have shot a hole the size of Colorado in your ass."

The first rule in arms safety was never to step into the path of a loaded weapon. What in the hell was his friend and business partner thinking? Of course, Jason had always run more on guts than strategy. Thankfully, he had the natural ability to pull it off.

His friend grinned. "Yours is about the only gun I'd dare step in front of."

Linc unloaded the weapon and slid the ammo magazine into his back jeans pocket. Jason walked with him toward the main building.

"You didn't answer my question," Jason said. "Oh, wait. Of course you didn't answer my question. You never answer my questions."

"Everything's fine."

Savage opened the door for him and he passed through. "Right. And if it wasn't, would you cop to it?"

Linc stared at him.

"Didn't think so." Savage followed him to the arms room. "I think that's the longest I've ever seen you spend on target practice."

Linc hadn't noticed the time passage. He'd merely experienced an intense urge to squeeze off a few rounds. To make himself feel useful.

And to stop thinking about how a certain sexy female had looked sleeping in her bed naked.

"Needed to put the time in," he ground out.

Jason wasn't known for asking a lot of questions. Especially ones he wasn't likely to get answers to. Which made his asking this one stand out.

Was his agitation that obvious?

Since Saturday night, when he'd left Regina asleep alone in her bed, he'd thought it a good idea to take a step back. And he had. He watched her as she went to work at the diner. He'd followed her to the library. And he'd tracked her remotely via his cell phone when he couldn't be near her.

Speaking of which, she should just be finishing up at the gym. He checked his cell. She was still there, but she wouldn't be for long.

"Hey, I was hoping to talk to you about something," Savage said, leaning against the prep table where Linc cleaned his weapon before putting it away in the rack against the wall.

"Shoot."

"Dangerous word to use, considering."

"Considering you stepped in front of my barrel, you mean?"

"That, too."

Linc cracked a smile.

He waited for Jason to get around to whatever he had to say.

Finally, his friend cleared his throat. "Look, you know everything that went down in Florida…"

Linc squinted at him.

It had been a great trip for the company, in that they'd found a crucial piece of information that kept the search for little Finley going. It had been bad, though, in that Savage had slept with Megan, a Lazarus partner who was another partner's girl.

"Anyway, things haven't exactly been, well, the same since…"

His words trailed off.

"Go figure," Linc offered.

Jason nodded his agreement. "Yeah. Which is why I'm thinking of maybe pushing up the date on opening that satellite office in Baltimore."

Linc finishing wiping down the M16 and placed it in the rack behind him.

"I haven't talked to anyone else about it. I thought I'd run it by you first, you know, see what you thought."

Linc faced him and crossed his arms over his chest. "How soon you talking?"

"Tomorrow too soon?"

They certainly had the resources for the expansion. Business income had already overshot their original forecasts by four hundred percent, and the next three months looked to double that again.

He checked his cell.

"Am I keeping you from something?" Savage asked.

Boy, he was really slipping when it came to keeping his thoughts to himself. First at the firing range, now with checking his cell phone. Of course, here he was surrounded by others trained in the art of observation, but he had the feeling he'd be just as transparent to an outsider.

"There's somewhere I need to be," he admitted.

Jason quirked a brow. "Need help?"

"I got it."

Jason pushed away from the table and slapped him on the shoulder. Savage was one of the few men Linc allowed such familiarity. Others risked physical injury even thinking about making such a move. "Well, think about what I said."

Linc gave his friend his full attention, considering the implications of his suggestion. "You're serious about this?"

"I'm serious about it."

Linc nodded. Then it seemed to him it was only a matter of time before it would happen…

7

REGINA CURLED HER legs under her on the love seat and called her mother again; again, there was no answer.

She left a second message and then sat for a long moment wishing she'd gone ahead and gotten that cell phone for her mother last Christmas. At least then, she'd be able to text her. Or if she was out somewhere, she could still reach her. Her mother was active, what with her job at the supermarket and volunteer work. But it was after ten on a Monday night. Where could she be?

She caught herself rubbing her arm and then looked toward the dark apartment window. The sun had long since set over the Rockies.

It would probably be a good idea to get to bed early. She had a long day ahead of her tomorrow with double shifts and classes. But she felt inexplicably restless. She went back to the living room and stared at her course books lying open on the coffee table. Then her gaze drifted to her silent cell phone. Before she knew what she was going to do, she had the phone in her hands and was pressing the name she'd entered yesterday morning.

But when Linc answered on the second ring, she hung up.

"Oh, good going, Ace. Like he doesn't know who called him."

Regina knocked the silent phone against her forehead and scrunched her eyes closed. Of course, there was always the chance he wouldn't call back…

The cell rang.

She took a deep breath and answered.

"Did you just call me?"

Regina bit her bottom lip and released it. "Um, yeah. Sorry. I don't know what happened."

Yes, she did. She hung up like the coward she was.

A quiet chuckle.

"Look, I, um, don't quite know how to say this but to come right out and say it. I'm sorry about the other night."

A heartbeat of a pause. "What for?"

She smiled. "Okay, then I'm not sorry."

"You may find this hard to believe, but women fall asleep on me all the time. I'm used to it."

It was her turn to laugh. "You're right. I do find that difficult to believe."

"Okay, then, I admit it. You are my first…in that regard," he said. "And that it's happened twice…well, a less confident man might take it personally."

"Well, good thing you're not a less confident man, then, isn't it?"

She enjoyed the moment of quiet flirting even as she slowly paced across the room.

She cleared her throat. "Um, you want to give it another shot?"

She started at the words the moment she said them.

Was she making a booty call? It was after ten o'clock and she was inviting a man over. A man she hadn't officially dated.

If it looked, smelled and sounded like one, it was a pretty good bet it was one.

Yes. Definitely a booty call.

"I don't know," he said.

The cringe turned to a wince. Bad enough to be making the call, but to get shot down once you did?

His chuckle tickled her ear. "I'm not sure even *my* ego could take a third time."

She briefly closed her eyes. "Oh, trust me, there isn't going to be a third time."

IT TOOK EVERY OUNCE of self-discipline Linc had not to get out of his SUV where he was parked in front of her building and walk the twenty steps to Regina's apartment.

He'd been going crazy all night watching her through the windows. First she'd eaten dinner. Then she'd studied. Then she'd called her mother and gotten no response before calling him.

He'd been startled when he'd watched her pick up her cell and then hear his own cell ring.

And he'd been exceedingly amused when she hung up.

He started the SUV and drove off. She'd likely be looking for him to pull up in about twenty minutes, so it wouldn't be a good idea to be seen getting out of a car that had been parked at the curb all night.

He didn't go far. He wasn't about to leave her place unprotected. So he drove a few blocks up and back-tracked, parking a little farther up her street out of eye-shot of her windows, but close enough for him to note any unusual comings and goings.

Twenty minutes later, he started the SUV up again and moved it back right in front of her place and got out.

Those twenty minutes ranked up there as some of the longest of his life.

Sex. Pure and simple. And the fact that he hadn't gotten it from her yet. That's what this was. Nothing more; nothing less.

He knocked on her door and she opened it imme-diately. The dampness of the ends of her curls and her change of clothes told him she'd taken a quick shower. The look in her eyes told him she'd been looking for-ward to this moment as much as he had.

She wore a simple pair of jeans that were anything but simple on her curvy frame, and a plain pink T-shirt that was anything but plain.

Damn, but she was beautiful.

And sexier than any woman had a right to be no matter what she was wearing.

He cleared his throat. "Hi."

She smiled. "Hi."

And then he was kissing her.

Linc wasn't clear on how he'd moved from point A to point B so quickly. All he knew was that one moment he was closing her apartment door and the next, he was pretty near swallowing her whole.

And she was eagerly returning his hungry attentions.

It seemed both of them were intent on making sure she didn't fall asleep again…

Damn, but she tasted good. Like toothpaste and hot female. And that she knew how to kiss was a bonus he'd already discovered but still marveled at. She had the type of mouth he could kiss for hours without paying any attention to time passage.

Well, normally. Right now, he knew a need so great to be buried deep inside her, he could concentrate on little other than reaching that destination pronto.

He palmed her breasts through the soft cotton, but it wasn't enough, so he tunneled his hands under the cotton before doing away altogether with the uncooperative material and the silky bra underneath.

Oh, yes…

She nicely filled his palms, the rose-colored tips stiff and pouty. He dragged his mouth from hers and bent to pull one of her nipples against his tongue. Her soft gasp filled his ears and her hands stilled on his back as he laved attention on her breasts.

He heard the pop of the buttons on his jeans and felt cooler air as she opened his fly. Still, he was unprepared when she slid her hand down the front of his Jockeys.

His breath hissed between his teeth when her hand wrapped around his erection.

It felt as if she was stroking his entire body with her fingers. When she might have dropped down to give him a repeat performance of their first night, he held her shoulders firm and kissed her instead. He was afraid if she put her mouth on him again, this would all be over before it started.

He unzipped her jeans and worked his fingers down between the soft denim and even softer skin, finding her as wet as he hoped she'd be.

Ready.

He scooped her up into his arms to her surprised giggle and carried her to the other room.

"What, foreplay done?" she whispered, kissing his neck.

"We've had four days of foreplay. I think it's time we finally got down to the main event."

"I couldn't agree more…"

He felt her shiver as he laid her down and made short work of the rest of her clothes and his. He was amused she'd not only left the box of condoms on the nightstand, but that she'd immediately opened a packet with her teeth and had one ready to sheath him with.

Linc gritted his teeth at the feel of the cool latex combined with her hot hands.

Then he nudged her knees apart and hovered over her, taking in the open want in her eyes as he bent down to kiss her…and then kiss her again.

He felt her hand on him again, this time guiding him to her waiting wetness. He paused, his heart beating an uneven rhythm in his chest as he entered her slightly. So tight…so hot…

She made a sound in the back of her throat and arched her back. He slowly entered her to the hilt, uncertain if the moan he heard at finally being joined together had come from her or him. Or a combination of both.

REGINA'S ENTIRE BODY burst into flame the instant he entered her.

A sigh began somewhere at the tips of her ears and traveled the length of her down to her toenails as she surrendered to the fire, gave herself over to it, allowed it to swirl in and around her, consume her every part.

Yes…

She'd felt, tasted the length and girth of him. But neither had prepared her for how wholly he filled her. His arms strained with the effort to keep himself above her. She wrapped her hands around his bulging biceps, wondering at his sheer size and strength. Then he stroked her again and she threw her head back, overcome with sensation. A long, deep moan drifted from her throat and it took her a moment to realize he was kissing her. She returned his lingering attentions, tangling her tongue with his even as their bodies tangled together in other ways, her legs curving around his, their hips coming together and apart, him inside her.

It had been so long since she'd felt such complete bliss. So connected to another human being. She was aware of the thick thrum of her heartbeat, the trembling of her womb, the essence of every part of him.

He drew back from the kiss and made a low sound in the back of his throat, urging up her own pleasure principle at the knowledge that she had done that…that they were experiencing this together. She slid her hands down over his chest, around his back and down to his behind, reveling in the feel of his movements even as she met him thrust for thrust.

His rhythm quickened, stealing her breath away. She moved her arms to brace herself against the mattress, trying to steady herself. Not only from the rocking of their bodies, but for the impending climax.

And then her hands were twisting in the bedsheets, the heat of the fire within her building unbearably high—until it exploded altogether…

8

THREE HOURS LATER, Regina lay back in bed, one word dominating her mind and one word only: *Wow!*

"I should have gotten a bigger box."

She heard Linc's voice, but it took her a moment to register what he'd said.

Condoms. He was talking about the box of condoms.

She smiled in lazy satisfaction and curved against him, feeling more liquid than solid. "Mmm."

He slid his arm around her and stroked her bare back from nape to bottom, making her feel like a contented cat.

"Well," he said.

She waited for the rest, watching as the headlights from a passing car shifted across the ceiling. "Well what?"

He chuckled softly. "Just...well."

His fingers played against her bottom and she found herself arching into his touch, inviting him to go as far as he dared.

"Worth waiting for?" she murmured.

"Oh, yeah."

She rolled to lie on her back and they both stared at the ceiling. She didn't know what had happened to the pillows or the top sheet. She didn't much care, either.

Every part of her tingled and shimmered, like the surface of a still pond someone had just thrown a stone into.

Stone? Try a boulder.

"How about you?"

She slowly turned her head to look at him, incapable of erasing the silly smile on her face. "How about me what?"

"Worth the wait?"

"Oh, yeah," she repeated his words. "In more ways than one."

His hand found her thigh and he rested it there, making lazy circles with his fingers. She liked that he wanted to keep touching her.

"How do you mean?" he asked.

Regina squinted at the ceiling. "Let's just say it's been a long, long time since I had sex."

"Me, too."

She laughed. "I think our concept of time may be a little different. I'm talking, um, years."

"Oh." He folded his other arm to support his head. She watched him, fascinated by his every move. "Years?"

"Mmm."

She wondered how he might interpret that. Would he think her frigid? Hard to get? Too busy? Or, worse, undesirable?

"You win," he said.

She laughed. "Hands down, I think."

A heartbeat of silence and then he asked, "Bad relationship?"

Regina's smile faded, but didn't disappear altogether. Which was a first. Usually when she reflected on that time in her life, it was difficult to find any reason to smile.

"Yeah," she said.

Her time with Billy had been like one long nightmare. She supposed in the beginning, things had been good. He'd been two years ahead of her in high school. She'd been flattered he'd even looked at her, much less demonstrated any interest in her. He'd asked her to his senior prom, took her for long rides on the back of his motorcycle. Her mother, of course, had never liked him. But like most girls her age, she hadn't listened to her mother. If anything, it had probably made her even more intrigued by the bad boy she was convinced had a heart of gold.

Her chest tightened at the memories.

"You haven't had sex since high school?"

Regina laughed so hard at the question, she was left with tears in her eyes. She hadn't been aware she'd spoken the words rather than merely thought them.

"And did he?"

"Did he what?"

"Have a heart of gold?"

She fell silent for a long moment. "No."

She'd ultimately determined his heart had been as black as coal and just as hard. But it had taken four years of living together after high school, multiple brushes with the law and a couple of physical altercations for her to finally admit her mother had been right.

"It's amazing what a female can forgive," she said quietly. "You know, if the guy has the right story."

In Billy's case, he'd been raised by an abusive, drunken father after his mother had disappeared when he was eight.

But when it was clear that rather than steering clear of the model his father had set, he'd instead followed it…well, she'd wanted out.

"Did you leave?"

"Yes. Across town. Got my own little apartment, a good job and started taking night courses."

Of course, Billy hadn't let her go that easily. He'd shown up on a regular basis at her place like a mewling cat in need of a bowl of milk. And, despite how much she wished she had done otherwise, she'd given it to him, believing him when he said she was the only person in the world he had. The only one who understood him.

"More like the only one stupid enough to believe everyone in the world deserves to have at least one person to trust."

Then came the bank robbery.

He'd been arrested before for armed robbery. He'd even served a short stint before his attorney had sprung him on a technicality. But this time people had been hurt. Killed.

When he was arrested, she'd been surprised at the relief she experienced that she'd no longer be responsible for Billy.

Responsible for him. That was, she'd come to understand, the way she'd felt.

Of course, he hadn't viewed his arrest as the end. He'd given her a list of things to do. And she'd done them. At least the ones that didn't require her having any interaction with him. She'd closed up his apartment and let his father know what had happened.

Then came his phone calls asking her to visit him.

She had. Once. To tell him it was over.

He'd been livid. He'd pounded the Plexiglas in the visitors' room trying to get at her. His response had surprised and terrified her.

His last words to her before guards dragged him away were, "I'm going to get you, you fucking bitch. You've betrayed me. When I get out of here, you're the first person I'm coming after."

She shivered now at the memory.

"Cold?" Linc asked.

He reached for the top sheet bunched at the foot of the bed and covered her.

How different Linc was. How thankfully, blessedly different.

She cuddled against him, absorbing his warmth, accepting his affection. "Thank you."

He slowly rubbed her back under the sheet. "You won't want to thank me when you hear what I have to say…"

THE FOLLOWING DAY, Linc couldn't believe he'd almost come clean about the true reason behind their meeting. He'd been a moment away from revealing he not only knew her ex and their situation, but that he'd been tailing her for the past week, hoping the SOB would show his face so he could send him straight back to hell where he belonged.

Then Regina had gazed up at him with those big green eyes and he'd choked, incapable of saying a word that would change the way she'd looked at him in that one moment.

He sat at the Lazarus conference table half listening to the meeting agenda move forward between his other five partners, kicking himself. Things were going to be difficult enough when Regina found out the truth. And he wasn't dumb enough to think that she wouldn't. He was convinced at some point—possibly very soon— Billy was going to turn up and then Linc would be forced to show his hand.

It wasn't going to be pretty. His thoughts went back to last night.

"What?" she'd said in the same drowsy, sexy voice she'd employed while sharing her past.

"Hmm?"

"What do you have to tell me? I hope it's not as ominous as it sounds."

She'd shifted closer to him, pressing her sex against the side of his leg in a way that made him forget everything but the need to feel her surrounding him again.

"We only have one condom left," he'd said, kissing her senseless.

"Linc? Does that get the green light from you?" Darius asked.

He blinked at his friend and partner, for the first time in a long, long time having missed what was said.

Damn. He was losing it.

The others seemed equally surprised as Dari repeated what he'd apparently missed and Linc gave his thumbs-up.

The meeting was drawing to a close. He glanced at Jason where he sat across from him. He raised a brow, as if to ask if now was the right time for the subject they'd discussed to be put on the table.

Jason gave a small shake of his head and then business was concluded.

Megan caught the exchange and looked between the two of them with open curiosity.

Now would have been the perfect opportunity for Jason to bring up the topic of pushing up plans for the opening of the Baltimore office. Why hadn't he done it? Linc gave an internal headshake. As far as he was concerned, there was no time like the present for seeing to business, unfinished or otherwise.

He grimaced. Right. If that was the case, then he should have come out and told Regina the truth last night.

As soon as the meeting was adjourned, Jason beat him to the door, disappearing down the hall before he could talk to him. Instead, Linc found himself next to Megan.

"What's up?" she asked as the others moved around them.

"With?"

She quirked a smile at him.

Megan was a beautiful woman. In more ways than one. And more than capable of holding her own against any man. He wouldn't dare presume to game play with her—she'd outmaneuver him easily.

"Something going on with Jason?" she asked.

Normally he might tell her to ask him. But in this case he knew that advice was faulty.

"We spoke about opening the Baltimore facility early."

Her brows rose. "Really?"

He didn't answer because he knew one wasn't required.

He also knew he didn't have to ask her not to say anything. His and Jason's conversation had not been in confidence. It had concerned business, no matter the personal motivation.

"I see," Megan said. "Thanks."

"Sure."

She began to drop back to enter a different part of the compound. "See you at the Barracks later?"

"Maybe."

She laughed and shook her head before turning around.

Linc checked his cell phone for Regina's location. She was still at the Beth El for classes, where she would be for the next hour or so before heading to work at the diner.

Of course, he didn't really need to check his locator for the information. She had casually told him her schedule this morning over breakfast.

He remembered the way she had looked, all dewy and pink from the shower, her hair up in a towel, wearing a University of Colorado T-shirt as she cooked up eggs and toast in her small kitchen. He'd felt himself harden all over again.

He had to remember to pick up more condoms later.

His cell phone rang as he reached the door to the parking lot. He recognized the number and answered after the second ring.

"What you got?"

"The subject in question suffered a home invasion seventy-two hours ago and is in ICU in an induced coma due to head trama."

He silently listened to the remainder of the report.

Damn.

Damn, damn, damn, damn.

He closed the cell phone and climbed into his SUV, wishing he had said something to Regina last night. Because then he could share the information that her ex had probably broken into her mother's place and nearly beat her to death…

9

REGINA CROSSED THE street from where she'd parked her car to the diner, watching for oncoming traffic. The hair standing up on the back of her neck had little to do with the honk of a car horn and everything to do with that uncomfortable sensation of being watched again.

She spotted a dark SUV parked up the way. Linc? She couldn't be sure. Dark SUVs were a dime a dozen in the military town.

Besides, what would he be doing there?

She half smiled to herself, last night returning to her in all its vivid glory.

Wow…

The word was still all that came immediately to mind whenever she thought of sex with Linc. What he could do with…well, everything—his mouth, his teeth, his hands and…other areas of his anatomy—was incredible. She ached in places she hadn't known existed… and sighed in others.

And having breakfast with him had seemed the most natural thing in the world.

How was it she hadn't realized how dull and gray

her life had become? Then again, maybe it took color to point out the contrast. And in that case, Linc was a vibrant, brilliant red.

She entered the diner to hellos from the owner, staff and some of the regulars and then crossed into the kitchen and the lockers in the back. The smell of fresh-brewed coffee and sizzling burgers teased her nose.

"You're early," Trudy remarked, leaning against the wall as she put her things in a free locker.

"Yeah, finished my errands earlier than I'd planned. Figured I'd do some class work before my shift started." She looked at her. "Unless you need me now?"

"No. We're good."

She smiled.

"I'll leave you to it, then."

Regina sat down on the bench and fished her cell phone from her purse. She dialed her mother's home number, received the dreaded answering machine again and then sat for a moment before calling Information for the number to the supermarket where she worked.

Seeing as it was a supermarket, and her mother worked as cashier, contacting her there wasn't something she'd ever done. Their conversations took place after she got home.

Within moments of getting the number from Information, she was on hold for the manager. When her call was finally answered, she introduced herself, which is as far as she got when the woman interrupted her.

"I'm so sorry about what happened, honey," the manager said. "When Deputy King stopped by yesterday to tell us the news, we were all in shock."

Regina's heart skipped a beat.

"I don't understand…"

Silence. "You don't know?"

Every unvoiced fear she'd had over the past couple of days lurched forward, making her dizzy. "Know what? I haven't been able to get a hold of my mother at home, so I called to see if I could catch her there."

"Oh, sweetie, I'm so sorry to be the one to break this to you. Your mother is in the hospital…"

LINC WATCHED AS REGINA rushed out of the diner as if the devil himself nipped at her heels. The sight of her surprised him because he'd just watched her go in a few minutes ago.

Now, she nearly ran straight into the stream of oncoming traffic, seemingly unaware of her surroundings. She looked spooked and anxious.

Linc got out of his SUV and hurried in her direction, meeting her when she made it safely across the road and was trying to find the right key to unlock her car door.

"Regina?" he said.

She looked at him but didn't seem to register him immediately.

"What is it?" he asked, gently taking her arms and turning her toward him. She dropped her keys and wildly tried to pick them back up, but he held fast, forcing her to look at him.

"What's wrong?"

"It's my mom," she said. "She needs me."

He glanced toward the diner where the owner and other staff stood in the window looking out at them.

He considered taking her there, surrounding her with people with whom she was familiar. Instead, he picked up her keys, handed them to her and steered her toward the park at the end of the block. She walked as if she was in a trance. Once there, he sat her on a bench and then took the spot next to her.

"Tell me what happened."

She did, outlining much of what he already knew. A part of him was relieved she'd received news of her mother without his having to tell her. But a larger part was afraid what she planned to do now.

Chances were, Johnson had tried to beat Regina's whereabouts out of her mother. And since she was in the hospital, odds were good he didn't get what he was looking for. So it was within the realm of possibility that she was left alive for a reason—Billy might be waiting for Regina to show up at the hospital.

Then again, there also existed the possibility that he'd gotten the information and was even now on his way to Colorado Springs.

"I've got to get to her…" Regina said, shivering despite the heat.

He put his arm around her and pulled her closer. "Did you talk to the doctor?"

She shook her head. "No, I spoke to a ward nurse. The doctor wasn't available."

"Did you leave a message?"

She nodded.

"I think it would be a good idea to wait to hear what he has to say before doing anything."

She nodded, but he wasn't sure she registered what he'd said.

They sat for a long minute silently, caught in a gauzy cocoon while the world continued to turn around them. Kids played on swings, an elderly woman walked by with one of those too-cute yippy dogs. Somewhere nearby the tinny music from an ice-cream truck sounded. Summer filled the air.

But all of it stopped just short of the air immediately surrounding them.

Regina's cell phone rang. She anxiously searched her purse before finding it in the pocket of her uniform.

"Hello?"

Linc waited, listening to her part of the conversation that was obviously with her mother's doctor.

"I see. Okay. Yes, yes, I'll call tomorrow."

She thanked him effusively and then slowly hung up the phone.

"He said she suffered severe head trauma and that he's induced a coma. She'll probably be under for at least the next forty-eight hours, when he'll assess whether she needs to be kept under longer."

Linc disguised his deep breath of relief.

"He said it wouldn't be any good for me to make the trip right now. She wouldn't know I was there anyway. But he'll call me daily with an update and they're not allowing visitors."

Thank you for sensible doctors.

They sat for a few more moments before he finally said, "Come on. Let me take you home."

It appeared to take an instant for her to interpret his words. "What are you doing here?"

He held her gaze.

Damn. He hadn't considered the consequences of his

actions when he'd rushed to her side. He'd only known an intense need to help her…to protect her from whatever she was experiencing.

"I'm sorry, that didn't come out the way I intended," she said quietly.

"That's okay. I was in the neighborhood checking on a job and I came to see if I could catch a cup of coffee with you over lunch," he said.

Was it him or did her questioning gaze linger a little longer than it should have? "Oh."

"Come on. Let's go."

She resisted. "But I have to work…"

"I'm sure they'll understand. How about we stop at the market on the way so we can buy the fixings and I can make you one of my world-famous Dagwood sandwiches?"

He got her walking back toward their cars. "World famous?"

"Yeah. You questioning my talents?"

The spark returned to her eyes. "And if I were?"

"Well, then, I guess I'll just have to prove it to you…"

THAT NIGHT, REGINA couldn't have said what would have happened had Linc not been there when she'd needed him. Her mother was the only family she had. If something happened to her…

She closed her eyes tightly. Something had happened to her. What remained was whether or not she'd pull through it all.

"Here. I didn't know if you took it with sugar, so I added some honey."

Regina opened her eyes to look at Linc. She accepted the cup of green tea and tried for a smile. "Thanks."

He sat down on the sofa next to her. His mere presence made her feel better. She didn't feel so alone.

As promised, earlier he'd made his sandwiches and she proclaimed that if they weren't already world famous, they should be. Of course, she didn't dare say she'd barely tasted the delicious meal. He even talked her into having a beer. That, combined with the shock, had made her drop straight off to sleep when he suggested she lie down for a bit.

Now, four hours later, he'd made her a big mug of green tea.

"Did you stay here the entire time?" she asked.

He easily stretched his arm across the back of the sofa. "No. I had some business to attend to. I used your key. I hope you don't mind."

She didn't. She sipped her tea and then smiled at him. "I guess that makes number three, then."

His expression was curious.

"Three times I've fallen asleep on you."

His chuckle touched her in places his hands had the night before. "Yes, but this time it was at my invitation."

"Ah. So then it's okay."

"Yes." He fingered her hair at the back. "How do you feel?"

"Curiously like I got hit by a truck."

"That's shock. Hopefully it'll pass by morning."

She nodded. "Part of your Marine training?"

"Something like that."

She sipped some more tea then placed the cup on

the table. "I feel like I should go home. Be by her side. Studies prove comatose patients are still aware of their surroundings."

"Naturally comatose patients. Not medically induced."

She knew that. Still, it didn't seem right somehow for her to be sitting here so far away while her mother was lying helpless in a hospital bed.

"Maybe you can call and ask a nurse to put the phone next to her ear. Speak to her for a few moments so she can hear your voice."

She felt her smile down to her toes. "Thanks."

He raised a brow. "For what?"

"For...well, for everything. I don't know what I would have done if you hadn't been there for me earlier."

"No thanks necessary. I'm just glad I could help."

She settled more comfortably into the sofa. Outside, the sun was dipping over the Rocky Mountains to the west. She hadn't turned on a lamp yet and the apartment was awash in golden-yellows and purples.

"Magic hour."

"Excuse me?"

She gestured toward the window. "That's what my mom always called this. You know...twilight."

She pulled her knees up to her chest, remembering Saturday afternoons spent, just the two of them, either hiking outdoors or browsing the library or baking. Her mother would tell her stories about her as a little girl and about her father.

Her favorite had always been about magic hour. It had been during one that her mother had known her father was meant for her.

They'd met when they were in their early twenties, doing what others their age did. Well, for the most part. Her mother was already working full-time at the supermarket. And her father was a Marine back on leave. They'd met while he was buying a box of condoms and she'd been the cashier to check him out. (Of course, Regina didn't find out what he'd been buying until she, herself, was twenty—her mother had said she hadn't remembered what he'd bought before that.) Her father had asked her mom out on a date, and she'd refused. Then refused the second time he asked. And the third.

The fourth she accepted.

They were supposed to go to a movie, but had lingered over hot dogs at a local drive-in place and then went for a long walk instead, talking about everything.

Then came Magic Hour.

It had been in that moment, as twilight fell, that she'd looked into Regina's father's eyes and known with everything she was that he was the one.

Regina sighed now. It hadn't been merely the story that had touched her, but the wistful expression on her mother's face every time she told it.

"It must have been hard on her when your father passed," Linc said quietly.

"Yes. She was devastated. She put up a good front for me, but…I always knew. When my dad died, a part of Mom died along with him."

She hadn't been aware she'd moved while she told the story, but now found herself curved against Linc's side, his arm around her, his breath soft against the top of her head. All she would have to do is look up and she'd be in perfect kissing position.

She did. They were. And he kissed her...

10

REGINA'S LIPS WERE the softest thing his mouth had ever tasted...

Linc tilted her chin up so he might kiss her more fully, amazed at the way his heartbeat sped up and his stomach tightened at the simple contact. Heat, sure and swift, rushed through him.

His cell phone vibrated against his hip.

Damn.

She laughed quietly. "Did the world just move? Or is that your cell?"

He cursed under his breath as he checked the display: Darius.

"I have to take this."

Regina slid over and he got up, pacing a few feet away before answering.

The last thing Linc wanted to do was leave Regina when she was feeling so vulnerable. But as he took the call, he knew he had to. He'd been neglecting his responsibilities over the past couple of days.

Why, then, was he feeling as if his responsibilities were out of whack and had been for a good long time?

"Can you look after it?" Darius asked. They'd run into a problem at a particularly popular downtown club where they supplied security personnel.

Generally there was no question. And there wasn't now. "Of course."

"Thanks, buddy. Call if you run into problems. Oh, wait a minute—I almost forgot who I was talking to. Of course there won't be any problems."

Words along those lines usually amused him. But not tonight. He closed his cell and stood for a long moment, his back to Regina. He didn't want to leave her.

He turned to find her with her own cell to her ear where she still sat curled up on the couch. He stood motionless, mesmerized by the sight of her.

"Mama? It's Reggie. How are you?" An awkward laugh. "Dumb question. I'm sorry you're in pain, Mama. The doctor says you're hanging in there. I need you to fight for me, you hear?" A long pause. "I was telling…a friend of mine about you and magic hour. About how you and Daddy first met. Remember? That was always one of my favorite stories…"

Linc felt oddly out of place listening to her side of the conversation. Which was interesting, considering he'd eavesdropped on nearly every one of her telephone calls over the past week, as well as knew her every move.

"Anyway," she said after sharing a couple of other memories. "I just wanted to tell you I'll see you soon. Get well. I love you, Mama."

Linc went into the kitchen where he could still hear her as she talked to the nurse, thanking her for holding the phone to her mother's ear and inquiring as to how everything was going. Apparently there was no change. Which could be a good or a bad thing. Only time would tell.

He filled a glass from the tap.

"You have to leave?" she asked from the doorway.

He emptied the bit of water he hadn't drunk and then placed the glass in the sink. "Yes."

"Will you be back?"

Her softly said question tugged at something that had nothing to do with sex, yet everything to do with it. "If you want me to."

She dropped her gaze and smiled. "I want you to."

"Then I'll be back."

He stepped in front of her, smoothing her hair from her face. Even without a lick of makeup she was still the most beautiful woman he'd ever seen. Especially without a lick of makeup.

He kissed her lingeringly.

Long minutes later, he groaned. "I better go or I might never get out of here."

She laughed quietly. "I'll try not to fall asleep while you're gone."

"If it's too late, I'll call first."

She shook her head. "No. Wake me."

Wake her.

He recalled the other night when he'd wanted to do just that. Now she was giving him permission to.

He let himself out of her apartment and strode toward his SUV, determined to get this job out of the way as soon as possible...

DARIUS HAD BEEN RIGHT to call him. The scene outside the Cave was utter chaos. Squad cars' flashing lights cast the rowdy crowd in white-and-red shadows. A popular national rock band that had just hit big had been scheduled to appear that night and the owner had requested extra personnel.

Apparently not enough.

Linc climbed out of his double-parked SUV and passed like a bullet through the crowd.

If outside was chaos, inside was hell. If everyone came out of this alive, they'd be lucky.

He slapped his hand on the shoulder of Dominic Falzone, one of Lazarus's top recruits.

"What's going on?"

"Damn crowd charged the building. A couple got trampled." He hooked a thumb over his shoulder where Linc made out a girl and a guy sitting on the floor of a hall leading to personnel offices while a paramedic attended to them. "We got the band out of here a half hour ago, but the people won't leave."

He scanned the overcrowded club interior. They were easily a hundred over capacity. The fire marshal was going to have the owner's balls in a vise if they didn't get them out before the police got a look inside the joint.

"You try the lights?"

"Of course. They only yelled louder."

Patrons were squeezed together, arms raised, chanting for the return of the band. A glance at the bar found waitresses standing on top of it, no room for them to maneuver on the floor.

"We stopped serving when we got the band out," Dominic said.

What an unqualified mess.

Still, in the madness swirling around him, Linc thought about calm and Regina. He wanted nothing more than to be back at her place right then, losing himself in her wetness…

The word caught and held his attention.

Dominic asked, "Shall we try crowd-control-scenario one?"

"No. Too large. We've got to get the crowd outside to disperse before even thinking about moving these guys out."

Dominic nodded. "What do you propose?"

"Band nearby?"

"Yeah. They're in a limo a few blocks up in case they can make it back in."

"That won't be happening. Get them back to their hotel. Then tell the limo to circle back here. Stop a block up."

Dominic squinted at him. "I don't understand."

"You will. Just do it." He patted him on the back and then made his way through the crowd toward the main bar where he conferred with the owner, sharing what he had in mind.

Fifteen minutes later, he got the call that the limo was parked outside.

"Good," he said to Dominic on his cell. "Now go outside and spark the rumor that the band is inside the limo…"

His plan worked as intended. The people waiting outside ran to meet the limo, leaving the area outside the club free.

As soon as he received the thumbs-up, Linc nodded for the owner and staff to leave.

Then he reached for the fire alarm, which activated a vigorous sprinkler system and loud alarm. He stood unblinking, watching as the crowd safely made its way for the doors, getting soaked in the process.

_11_

REGINA COULDN'T BE sure how much time had passed when she blinked her eyes open to the darkness of her bedroom. It could have been minutes, it could have been hours. She moved and the novel she'd been reading fell onto the floor. She frowned at it. Damn. She'd fallen asleep. Again.

The clock told her it was after eleven.

She swung her legs over the side of the bed, still fully dressed. That's funny. She'd been reading so she'd had the lamp on. She couldn't remember switching it off.

She heard a sound from the other room. Goose bumps rushed up one arm and over to the other.

Linc?

For reasons she couldn't fully form, she had the sinking sensation it wasn't him. For one thing, he never seemed to make a noise when he moved. Which said a lot considering how big he was. For another, there were no lights on anywhere in the apartment insofar as she could tell. And she definitely remembered leaving one on so Linc could see when he came back.

She quietly got up from the bed, cringing when the bedsprings gave a quiet groan.

Silence.

Had she been imagining things? Could the sounds have come from the next apartment rather than inside hers? Or was someone outside perhaps working on their car?

She stood stock-still, listening, hoping she could hear any noise over the sound of her own hammering heartbeat.

There! Definitely a sound coming from the other room.

Her breathing sounded loud in her own ears. She looked around for something with which to whack the unknown visitor. She found nothing short of the lamp. And even that was too big and unwieldy to consider using.

Taking short, measured steps, she tried to recall her self-defense classes, but all that came to mind were the boxing techniques she'd learned most recently. To keep from hurting herself, she silently removed her rings and stuffed them into her front jeans pocket.

She stopped to the side of the doorway, gathering her wits about her and drawing in a silent breath. Then she peeked around the side, trying to make out shapes in the other room.

A figure stood near the window apparently going through her books.

Linc? No. This person was shorter, smaller, but obviously a man.

She eased back against the wall and closed her eyes. What to do, what to do, what to do…

Her cell!

She stared at the bedside table where the phone lay. She ordered her legs to take her to it so she could call 911. But the limbs refused to cooperate.

Then, as she watched, the instrument lit up and gave a shrill ring.

Regina's heart nearly leaped from her chest.

She charged the nightstand even as noises grew louder from the other room. She fumbled with the phone, noting Linc's name in the display before hearing her front door slam.

"Hurry!" she shouted upon answering. "There's someone in the house!"

LINC WANTED TO PUNCH something. He didn't care what. Just so long as he could experience the satisfaction of his fist hitting a hard surface.

He'd been three blocks away when he'd made the phone call to Regina to check if she still wanted him to come over, but it might as well have been three miles. He'd stepped on the gas, but by the time he arrived, whoever had been in her apartment was long gone and she was on the phone with 911.

Now, an hour later, the responding officers had just left and Linc was so upset he didn't think he could sit down.

"Thanks for coming so quickly," Regina said quietly from where she stood leaning against the doorway to the kitchen rubbing her arms.

He hadn't come quickly enough, to his way of thinking.

In fact, he should have never left.

He glanced around at the mess the intruder had made. Books were strewn over the floor, her sofa had been slashed, two plants had been turned over.

"I wonder what he was looking for," she whispered.

He knew what the guy was looking for, namely, the money from the bank robbery. Moreover, he knew exactly who the guy was.

He searched her spooked face, wishing he could erase the fear there.

He didn't need to ask her any questions. The police had done that while he listened. Even if he hadn't heard her answers, he wouldn't have needed to say a word.

She'd left the door unlocked for him.

Instead, Billy Johnson had used it to gain access to her apartment…

He was thankful she didn't appear to know it had been Johnson. A thought that left him with mixed feelings.

"Do you keep any valuables in the house?" he asked. "Anything anyone would know about?"

Her hand fluttered to the side of her throat. He followed the movement, wanting to place his mouth where her fingers touched. "I don't have any valuables." She gestured toward the small LCD television that was no larger than a computer monitor. "He didn't even touch the TV."

Of course "he" hadn't. Mostly because "he" had been looking for the money he was convinced she'd taken from him.

Linc moved toward the door.

"Where are you going?" she asked, pushing away from the wall anxiously.

"The applicable question is, where are we going?"

"And the answer?" she asked as she gathered her purse, which had been rifled through.

"To Lazarus to pick up some security equipment I can install."

"Tonight?"

"Tonight."

Her smile was faint, her gratitude evident as she preceded him through the open door.

IT WAS WELL after 3:00 a.m. She'd sat in Linc's SUV while he'd gone inside an impressive compound just outside town and then they'd returned to her place. While she cleaned up, he installed a dead bolt on her door, some sort of complicated locks and sensors on her windows, and an alarm system with a security code she had to key in every time she came and went. She couldn't imagine how much the sophisticated equipment would cost on the open market, but she did offer to pay him in installments for the value. He'd refused.

So she'd gone about showing her appreciation in a completely different way…

Now, after two hours of hot sex, they lay back in bed, Regina finding it almost impossible to believe just a short time ago she'd been terrified, afraid she'd never feel safe in her own apartment again.

She stretched from where she lay stomach down against the mattress, running her bare leg against his, her sex swollen and on fire…and hungry for more.

She'd never experienced this sort of insatiable desire

for someone before. No matter how long they went, she wanted more. And still more after that.

"Damn, what you do to me," he murmured as if hearing her thoughts.

She hummed her response and leaned her hip against his. She felt boneless, completely and utterly satisfied.

She felt his hand on her bottom, the heat of his touch radiating everywhere.

Oh, boy…

She wiggled suggestively.

"You can't possibly want more." His voice was rough.

She hummed again.

"Aw, hell…you're going to be the death of me…"

His hand nudged toward the apex of her thighs from behind and she caught her breath. "Yeah, but what a way to go, huh?"

Linc rolled toward her and up to all fours. He sheathed himself, nudged her knees apart with his and then grasped her hips. She all too willingly lifted to her knees, sighing when she felt his tongue against her back, igniting tiny little flames everywhere it lapped. She stretched her neck, giving him access to the nape. He bit down slightly and she gasped, the chance to catch her breath denied her when he positioned himself against her from behind.

She moaned, wanting him inside her. A wish he didn't immediately grant her as he curved a hand around her hip and found her clit from the front, giving a gentle pinch.

Regina threw her head back and raised so her arms supported her, giving her the leverage she needed to bear back against him. But rather than give her what she wanted, he compensated for the move, continuing to stroke her from the front and run the thick, hard length of his erection between her swollen folds from behind.

She swallowed hard, her entire body seeming to tremble from head to foot.

"Please…" Her voice sounded foreign to her own ears.

She rocked forward and back in rhythm to his strokes, attempting to force entrance whenever the tip of his erection rested near the core of her wetness.

Finally he repositioned himself where she wanted to feel him most and entered her slightly.

She moaned in sweet abandon…then groaned when he withdrew again.

By the time he entered to the hilt, her womb contracted and she reached crisis level. But rather than stop, Linc continued his deep strokes, drawing out her orgasm and coaxing her back to join him.

Regina had never felt so possessed by something larger than herself. So at the mercy of her emotions, sheer, blissful sensation. She barely recognized herself in the woman she'd become, one given over to abandon, unfettered, unleashed.

She lifted until she was kneeling, reaching behind her to grasp Linc's hips. She turned her mouth into his kiss, the world little more than a hazy red cloud around them.

Linc took advantage of her new position, curving one hand up to cup her breast, the other to stroke her externally even as he continued internally.

Regina never wanted it to end…never wanted him to withdraw…to stop. She wanted them to remain as they were, right that moment, forever.

He rocked into her even as she arched into him, tension swirling and tightening deep in her belly, with each pinch of her nipple, every flick of her clit, the shear sensation of him filling her.

He groaned into her ear, his hand coming up to cup her chin possessively, holding her still as his rhythm increased. She arched her back to allow him deeper access. And when he came, she came with him.

_12_

WHAT IN THE hell was he doing?

Linc had spent the day juggling his Lazarus duties with tailing Regina and felt as raw as an overworked piece of meat. Right now she was covering the dinner shift at the diner and due to get off soon. He was heading to her place, where he planned to add a motion sensor to the other equipment he'd already installed.

He gripped the steering wheel so tightly he had to consciously loosen it for fear he'd snap it clean off.

Last night had been…incredible. But having hot sex with Regina was the last thing he should be doing right now.

Yeah? Easy to say that now that he'd spent all night doing it.

He could virtually hear his back teeth grinding together. With the break-in interrupted yesterday, it was a pretty good bet that Billy Johnson was already plotting ways to finish the job. He had the bedroom yet to search.

And that angered Linc all the more. What had Johnson planned to do once he'd completed going through the living room while Regina was asleep?

The possibilities brought his blood to the boiling point.

Damn it, he should have told her. He should have let her in on the fact that her ex had broken out of prison. Better she should be aware and prepared than continue allowing her to stumble around in the dark a moment longer.

His reasons were purely selfish at this point. While he might have explained away his duplicity before as a business matter, now...well, now that Johnson was in the area and had made his first move, Regina's ignorance placed her in greater danger.

And once she did know? What would she do? What would the revelation that her ex was not only in her area, but after her, compel her to do? Would she run yet again?

The idea sent something awfully similar to fear stabbing through his chest as clean as an ice pick.

Then there was what Johnson might have up his sleeve to consider. Once he discovered Regina didn't possess what he was looking for...

He had no doubt physical confrontation would be next.

Linc thought of Regina's mother lying in a medically induced coma halfway across the country and tightened his fists on the steering wheel again. He tried to find comfort in the thought that there was still one step Johnson had yet to take—finish his search of Regina's apartment—before he reached that point. But the knowledge was of little consolation.

Linc had to put all this together to make a workable resolution. Now.

And pray that it didn't end up with his getting kicked out of Regina's life.

Life?

No, her bed.

He parked his truck and then let himself into her place with the spare key she'd given him so she wouldn't have to leave the door unlocked again. Not that she could do that anymore, not with the system he'd installed. If she didn't lock the door, it would automatically lock within two minutes of being closed. That was another reason she'd insisted he take an extra key, and he'd suggested she have a copy made to keep elsewhere, say, in her locker at work, just in case she accidentally locked herself out.

The instant he entered her place, he felt different. The tension coiling his muscles eased a bit. Merely being surrounded by her things, her scent, made him feel better. Even without her there, he could at least sense the anticipation that she would be soon.

He dropped his duffel on the floor and went to the kitchen to put away the bag of groceries he'd picked up. Sandwich fixings, juice, eggs and a loaf of bread.

His cell rang. He glanced at the display. It was his aunt.

"Hey, kiddo," she said when he picked up.

He smiled slightly. He'd tried asking her once to stop calling him that, considering it had been a long time since he'd been a kid. She'd told him that to her, he would always be the quiet little boy who stole her heart, so he might as well prepare himself to hear the endearment when he was sixty, granted she lived long enough to still be calling him that.

"Hey, yourself, Aunt Rose. How are you doing?"

"I'm good. Better now I've heard your voice. There was a ruckus up the block last night. A fire. They evacuated everyone on this side of the street and fire-truck lights made it feel like day instead of night. But so long as my place is still here, and my plate of fried chicken still on the counter, I figure everything's good."

Somehow she always made him feel as if he'd just left her place after a big meal. He could almost smell her fresh biscuits baking in the oven. "Glad everything's okay. Anyone get hurt?"

"No, no. Thank goodness. But Val is shopping for a new place. Told her that's what she gets for leaving her curling iron plugged in. Anyway, she's bunking with me until we can get her set up somewhere else."

"A curling iron?"

"Mmm-hmm. She swears a girl never knows when she'll need a quick curl. Learned her lesson the hard way."

He chuckled and then said, "Sorry I missed your call last night."

"Apology accepted. So long as there's a good reason for it."

He looked around the apartment, but didn't comment.

"You know, like a girl?"

"I'm too old for girls."

"A guy is never too old for girls."

"Good point."

A pause and then, "Okay, what's her name?"

He moved into the other room to get his equipment out of his duffel. "What's whose name?"

"Boy, I know you better than you know yourself. Who is she and when do I get to meet her?"

Considering his aunt hadn't met anyone he'd dated since he was in high school, he had to give her credit for never losing faith. Hell, it was all he could do to get back home for a visit every few months. He couldn't imagine arranging for someone to go with him.

Or at least he couldn't before.

Now...

"That serious, huh?"

"What?"

"Whenever you go quiet, it means something important."

"I'm always quiet."

"Yes, but not in this way quiet. Is she pretty? I bet she is."

"She looks just like you, Aunt Rose."

That made her laugh. "Lord, I hope not."

"I told you the woman I end up with would have to be just like you, or else she wouldn't be worth having."

Silence. As much from her as from him.

Had he really just said what he had? Did he consider Regina his girl?

He dry washed his face with his hand, hoping his aunt had missed the slipup, even as he knew she wouldn't. Not in a million years.

"What's her name?" she asked. "And when are you bringing her home to meet me?"

He looked around, for a moment forgetting what he

was there to do. "Look, Aunt Rose, I'm on a job. I've got to run."

"Don't you dare hang up this phone, Lincoln," she said.

"I don't want to. I have to."

"Promise you'll call me later."

"I promise I'll try to call you later."

A long sigh and then, "Fine. But be prepared to share something when you do, kiddo. You can't leave an old woman hanging like this. It's not good for the heart."

He chuckled. "You're not old and your heart's fine."

They said their goodbyes and he pocketed his cell phone just as he heard voices outside the front door. He was getting to his feet when Regina entered, her friend Vivienne on her heels.

REGINA WAS SURPRISED to see Linc inside her apartment. If she'd known he was there, she wouldn't have invited Vivienne over for a late supper.

"Linc," she said softly.

She recovered her composure, but she was sure it wasn't in time for Viv to catch it.

"Well, well, well. What do we have here?" Her friend made no attempt to disguise her open appraisal of the man standing over a duffel full of equipment.

"Viv," Linc said. "How are you?"

She stepped farther inside and around him, still giving him the once-over. "I think the applicable question here is how are you? If I were going by looks, I'd say fine. Very fine, indeed."

Regina gave an eye roll, her friend's flirting rubbing her the wrong way.

Linc cleared his throat and met her gaze. "I stopped by to install those motion sensors I told you about."

"Oh," she said.

"Mmm...motion sensors." Viv hooked a finger under the short sleeve of his black T-shirt and tugged. "I could suggest a few motions the three of us might make."

"Viv!" Regina was aghast.

"I think that's my cue to leave," Linc said.

Regina nearly sighed with relief. Then she realized how rude it was to allow him to go just because her friend couldn't behave herself.

"No, no. Please, finish," she said. She raised a bag. "I brought a few rib eyes from the diner. Stay for supper?"

"Mmm...yes. He can be dessert."

Regina grabbed her friend's arm and maneuvered her into the kitchen. "Actually, I'm going to have you make dessert."

"I'd much rather have him."

As soon as they were in the kitchen and she'd put the bag down, out of Linc's earshot, she said, "What are you doing?"

Viv appeared amused. "What do you mean what am I doing? I'm taking up where we left off the other night."

"Yeah, well, stop it."

Viv looked her over, but in a different way than she had Linc.

Regina wasn't clear why she hadn't told her friend she and Linc had been seeing each other. She'd even left out his involvement last night, saying only that she'd had a security system installed, mentioning nothing about who had installed it.

Scratch that. She knew exactly why she hadn't told Viv about Linc: because of exactly what was happening now.

"Wait a minute…" Viv said. "You two have been seeing each other?"

Regina turned toward the bag and took out the paper-wrapped steaks she'd gotten from the diner.

Viv came to lean on the counter next to her. "Why didn't you say anything?"

Regina shrugged. "I don't know. It never came up."

"Never came up." Viv crossed her arms and leaned closer. "I hope that's the only thing that never came up."

"God, you can't help yourself, can you?" Regina laughed.

"Sorry, it's just the way I'm made." Her voice dropped to a whisper. "So, how…big is he?"

13

IF SHE'D HOPED her talk with Vivienne during dinner preparations would help defuse her friend's outrageous behavior, she'd been sadly mistaken.

Dinner was awkward at best. Regina was convinced Vivienne couldn't help herself when it came to good-looking men. Which might explain why she couldn't seem to keep female friends. She complained that whenever her friends hooked up with a steady guy, they stopped talking to her. Could this be one of the reasons?

Regina knew a bit of Viv's past, but not nearly enough to pass judgment, nor to help her in any meaningful way. She should probably make an effort if she hoped to give their friendship a good shot at making it over the hurdle that seemed to doom her other friendships.

As it was, it was all she could do to keep Viv from climbing into Linc's lap to demonstrate why she thought it was a good idea that the three of them revisit the other night, preferably without alcohol and with sex.

It got so bad halfway through the meal, Linc made a

show of checking his cell phone and excusing himself from the table, saying he had to leave.

Regina got up to see him out.

When Viv moved to do the same, Regina caught her shoulders where she sat in the kitchen chair and held her in place. "I've got this. Stay and finish your meal."

"I'd much rather see if I can sample some dessert."

"I'd much rather you didn't."

Thankfully her friend finally seemed to take the hint and stayed where she was. Still, Regina wasn't taking any chances. Rather than saying goodbye to Linc inside the apartment, she stepped outside with him, soundly closing the door behind her.

"Shit," she said as the bolt automatically hit home. "I forgot my keys."

Linc jingled his.

She smiled.

"Looks to me like your friend has a few issues," he said quietly.

She searched his face, looking for a trace that any of the attention Viv had bestowed on him was welcome. "Well, you did come home with both of us the other night."

He nodded and looked down at their feet.

The thought was a sobering one for her, as well. It was easy enough to forget when the two of them were alone together. But with Viv present…well, it cast whatever might or might not be happening between them in a slightly different light.

Slightly? An entirely different light.

"I'm not done installing the motion sensors," he said.

She looked over her shoulder at the closed door.

"I was thinking maybe you could come stay the night at my place tonight," he said.

The idea made her heart dip low in her chest.

"You know, just to make sure you're safe."

She smiled. "Is that the only reason?"

His eyes were full of naughty suggestion.

And if it weren't for her friend inside the apartment, and the reminder that they had started out as a threesome that had ultimately continued in a twosome…

"I think I just want to be by myself tonight."

She wanted time to think.

He seemed to search her face with the same intensity with which she'd looked into his moments earlier.

"I'm not sure how I feel about that," he said.

She squinted at him.

"The security system isn't fully functional right now."

"And the chances someone's going to break into my apartment again so soon after the last time?" she asked, amused.

He fell silent.

"Look, I don't mean to sound ungrateful. Thank you for all you're doing…"

"No thanks necessary," he said.

She briefly bit her bottom lip. "I just think it's a good idea if I get some sleep tonight. If we *both* get some sleep tonight."

He chuckled at that, and awareness spread like warm honey throughout her stomach. A moment longer and she was pretty sure she might change her mind.

PROBLEM WAS, LINC had no intention of getting any sleep. Worse, he wouldn't have Regina's luscious body next to him to keep him awake.

He climbed into his SUV and drove around for a while before heading back and parking up the street from Regina's apartment. She'd given him a lingering kiss that had left him more than a little hot and bothered before he'd unlocked the door so she could go back inside.

Vivienne…

He cursed under his breath. If anything were capable of cooling him off, it was thoughts of her during dinner. She'd been almost vulgar in her come-ons, as about discreet and subtle as a ten-dollar whore. Oh, he'd dealt with her type often enough. But by the horrified expression on Regina's face, he got the feeling that she not only hadn't, she hadn't known her friend was capable of the behavior.

Of course, Vivienne had been oblivious to it all. Which had made her naked advances all the more awkward.

Damn.

He settled back more comfortably in the chair…comfortably being a relative term. He didn't like the brassy redhead monopolizing Regina's time.

Of course, if it hadn't been for Vivienne, the two probably wouldn't have met.

Then there was how close he felt to something resembling jealousy.

Was he jealous of Regina's friend?

Yes, he realized, he was. He'd be envious of anything that took her time away from him.

New to him.

He watched a car come up the street behind him and slow its speed. He picked up his advanced cell phone and focused on the plate. Local. It pulled to a halt near Regina's building and someone got out of the passenger's seat. A woman. The car continued and Linc watched as the woman walked to a house across the street and let herself in.

One of Regina's neighbors. An art-gallery secretary who lived in the three-bedroom house with her husband and one child. He watched through the open front window as the six-year-old boy launched himself into his mother's arms and the husband got up from the sofa to welcome his wife home.

Surveillance of this nature required not only watching the subject in question, but also the people who surrounded them, as well. Someone like Billy Johnson wouldn't hesitate to use any of Regina's neighbors in order to gain access to her. Up to and including those she worked with at the diner.

In fact, this morning he'd figured he'd put more man-hours into this case than he had any in recent memory, up to and including the assignment around the missing girl in Florida. Of course, then, because of his status as an ex-FBI agent and his continuing contact with the Bureau, he'd acted more as a liaison and worked as part of a team. He was on his own on this one. Which is how he preferred it. At least when it came to Billy Johnson.

He wished the escaped con would slip up, show his face and let Linc nab him already.

And once he did? Would Regina still want anything to do with him?

He rubbed his face with his hands, the question tailing him like his shadow day in and day out.

She said she'd felt responsible for Johnson. How would she feel if she knew he was the one to send him back to prison? While Linc was confident she didn't harbor any romantic feelings for the man, the other almost maternal instincts tended to be a little more deeply ingrained.

Then there was the little matter of his own dishonesty.

Little?

At this point it was coming to resemble the Rocky Mountains behind him.

He sighed and shifted in the seat again, watching Regina's living room window, tracking the two shadows there as they moved from the kitchen to the sofa and chairs. What were they talking about? he wondered. Of course, all he'd have to do to find out was switch on the receiver to the listening devices he'd installed his first night there. But he had a feeling he wouldn't want to hear what they were saying.

And he certainly didn't want to know what Vivienne was saying.

"Damn," he said aloud.

This was going to be a long night...

14

"I'D LIKE you to come out with me tonight."

Recalling Linc's words, said during a cell-phone call in the middle of the lunch rush, was enough to make Regina feel as if she'd gotten a good night's rest. And a new pair of feet.

Neither of which she had, of course.

After working a double shift, she ached in all the wrong places.

And last night, she'd tossed and turned. If she wasn't thinking about Linc and how much she wished he were next to her, Viv was intruding in her thoughts, sharing things she wasn't all that sure she'd wanted to know.

While she'd heard stories about women relocating to Colorado Springs solely for the purpose of meeting, dating and ultimately marrying air force pilots, she'd never actually met one…until Vivienne. Of course, she hadn't learned that until now. She'd learned her friend had been through two pilots already, both relationships ending in dismal failure. Even odder, it seemed Viv was only concerned that the tight-knit military community would saddle her with the reputation of being a groupie.

As for Linc...

How was it, in such a short time, she had a difficult time imagining what life had been like without him? Thoughts of him began the moment she woke in the morning and followed her throughout the day. He even invaded her dreams. She reviewed the things she did know about him and imagined the answers to things she didn't.

Then there was Viv...

How was it they had been friends for over a year and had never really talked? Oh, they'd spoken. But not about anything important. Not about what really mattered. She supposed part of the reason was because she, herself, had so much to hide. She'd told no one about her past. About Billy. She talked about her mom often enough, but everyone did that.

Well, everyone but Viv.

Regina sat down on the bench in the diner employees' area and absently untied her shoes. She'd asked about Viv's parents once. And had received a noncommittal answer. She'd easily dismissed the incident, not thinking anything of it, when perhaps she should have.

No, she definitely should have.

She took off her shoes one by one and replaced them with her sneakers.

Of course, there was no way she could have known the truth, much less guessed at it.

Linc...

She experienced what was akin to a full-body sigh again. Then looked at her watch. Shoot! She had only forty-five minutes to get home, shower and get ready before he came to pick her up.

She grabbed her things and headed for the door, her feet and heart feeling light again.

SMOOTH MOVE, SLICK.

Bringing Regina to the Barracks had been a bad idea. But since he hadn't been about to leave her at home alone, and he couldn't miss Jason Savage's birthday celebration, he'd figured it was the only viable solution.

If only his partners and coworkers weren't staring at him as if he were a few cards short of a full house, he might never have questioned his thought processes.

He glanced at Regina. If she noticed anything out of whack with their open surprise, she easily hid it, her smile wide and warm. He'd suggested she dress casual when she'd asked what she should wear, and she had in a simple pair of jeans and a purple blouse that hugged her curves nicely.

He introduced everyone and she shook hands with them, one by one.

"And this is the birthday boy," Darius said, indicating where Jason sat next to him.

"Happy birthday," Regina said easily, shaking his hand.

"Thanks, Regina. Nice to meet you." His grin was wider than usual as he looked them both over. "*Very* nice to meet you."

Oh, he was going to hear it for this one, Linc knew.

He'd never brought a date to anything. In fact, he made it a point of going out of his way to avoid any kind of fix ups altogether whenever in the company of his professional team.

Of course, Regina wasn't really his date.

Damn.

Who was he kidding? He took in the way she laughed, registering how merely being near her made him feel, and realized the only person he seemed to be fooling was himself.

Thankfully, everything settled down into an uncomplicated rhythm after the introductions. He and Regina sat at the table reserved in the back for the occasion. She chatted easily with Megan and the guys, and sipped on the draft beer poured from one of the pitchers ordered for the table. Which was more than he could say for himself. He kept looking at his cell, estimating how soon he could get out of there.

Then he blinked and the table seemed to undergo some sort of silent version of musical chairs. Suddenly three people appeared between him and Regina, with Jason sitting to his right.

He got up, deciding to go to the restroom to wash his hands, and Jason got up with him.

"Hey, there," his friend said, catching up with him. "Got a minute?"

"No."

Jason's full-throated laugh set his back teeth on edge. "I'm the birthday boy, remember? You're not allowed to tell me no."

Linc stared at him.

"So…who's the chick?"

Linc lengthened his stride and Jason matched it. "She's not a chick."

"Oh, I see."

"Tell me, Savage, what exactly do you see?"

His friend looked a little too amused for his liking. "A lot more than what you're likely willing to tell me."

"Such as?"

"Such as…you like her."

Linc pushed in the men's-room door with more pressure than was necessary, nearly taking out a guy who was on his way out. He apologized without looking at him.

"And she likes you."

"She isn't my date."

They took their spots at the urinal.

"Well, if she isn't, then what is she?"

"She's…"

Revealing who she was would be tipping his hand when he wasn't quite ready to.

Simply, he didn't want his team knowing what he was up to. Billy Johnson was his personal target; he didn't want backup. Didn't need it. And he didn't want anyone to know just what it was that made it personal.

Then there was the fact that Regina was more than Johnson's old girlfriend. Far more. Even if the only reason he had brought her along tonight was related to Johnson.

He finished up and stepped to the sink.

"I like her," Jason said next to him.

Linc slanted him a glance. "I'm happy for you."

"What would you say if I asked to date her?"

Linc turned toward his friend so quickly, Jason

instinctively took a step back, raising his dripping hands.

"Whoa, big guy, slow down." He looked at where Linc's hands were fisted at his sides and then reached for a couple of paper towels from a dispenser behind him, handing Linc one. "Just making a point."

"Oh? Well, you had better spell it out for me before I make you eat this paper towel."

Jason laughed so hard Linc was tempted to make him eat the entire dispenser.

"I'm sorry. I didn't mean to laugh. Please don't take offense..."

"If you don't stop..."

Jason raised his hand again. "Hey, I'm just pointing out you've got feelings for the girl. That's all. And if you have feelings, well, that makes her your date."

"Who said I have feelings?"

"Who?" Jason pressed a finger into his chest. "You. By looking like you wanted to bash my head into the sink for daring to ask what I did."

"Yes, well, at least you asked permission this time."

If any words were capable of sobering his friend up, those were it.

They stood staring at each other for long moments, neither of them needing to be reminded of what had gone down in Florida.

The door opened and Darius stepped in.

"What's up?" he asked, elbowing between them to use one of the sinks.

"Nothing," Jason ground out before leaving the room.

Dari met Linc's gaze in the mirror. "What he said," Linc offered.

Then he left as well, leaving Darius appearing puzzled behind him.

"NEVER?" REGINA WHISPERED in response to Megan's comment.

"Never. Ever. In fact, some of the guys were beginning to wonder if he was...well, you know."

"Gay?"

Megan nodded.

Regina smiled so wide it almost hurt her face. "Trust me, he's not."

"I figured as much."

Regina liked the woman who had come to sit next to her after Linc had left the table. She understood she was one of Linc's partners and immediately picked up on her connection to Darius, another partner.

She wasn't sure what she'd expected when Linc had invited her out. Perhaps dinner or a movie, or even a night dancing at a club, not unlike the one where they'd met, despite his suggestion she wear casual clothes.

But this kind of outing wasn't even on her radar.

What did it mean that he was introducing her to his friends and business associates?

She caught sight of him as he returned to the table. His expression was thunderous. And the partner whose birthday it was, Jason, looked more sober than the beer she'd seen him drinking would suggest.

She watched Megan look between the two men, her brow wrinkling. Regina immediately picked up on something going on. An undercurrent of tension she didn't understand.

And that was probably none of her business.

But she couldn't help wondering, nonetheless.

Linc had spoken a little of his past. Of his aunt and the Bronx. But when it came to his business or personal relationships, he'd said very little. Heck, she hadn't even been aware that they were meeting up with his friends tonight, and that it was in honor of one of their birthdays. It might have been nice to know that.

Had he always been so quiet? If so, she wondered why.

A guy she'd seen behind the bar pulled up a chair next to her.

"Hey, Jax," Megan said warmly, her pretty face softening. "Meet Regina. She's Linc's date. Regina, this is Jason's younger brother, Jackson."

They briefly shook hands. "Linc?"

Regina looked down, suddenly feeling awkward.

"I'm sorry. Didn't mean to make you uncomfortable."

"No, no. It's okay. We haven't been...dating long."

Actually, she wasn't entirely certain that's what they had been doing. While he'd stopped by the diner and they'd enjoyed a couple of meals together, tonight was the first time he'd actually asked her out.

Of course, there was the sex.

Regina was glad Jax and Megan were engaged in conversation and weren't looking at her face, which she was afraid might reveal more than she cared to consider.

"Hey, Jax," Jason said from across the table. "You and Megan have absolutely nothing to talk about."

Conversation stopped as the younger man looked at his brother.

More awkwardness.

Regina guessed there was a lot more going on within this group than she could ever hope to figure out in a single night. So she resolved not to try.

But Jackson held up his hands, said his goodbyes to Megan, said it was nice to meet her and left the table.

Megan leaned closer. "Never mind all that. Jax's been angling for a job at Lazarus forever, but Jason doesn't want him there. Long story."

Regina smiled at her and took a sip of her beer, searching for a way to change the subject. "He work here?"

"For now, yes."

Instead, she looked to find Linc rising to his feet. She gazed at him hopefully.

A simple nod of his head told her he was ready to go...

15

LINC COULDN'T HAVE ushered Regina from the bar quickly enough.

What the hell was all that?

If he'd had a clue that any of that would have gone down the way it had, he would never have brought Regina here.

Hell, he wouldn't have come himself.

His partners might be the closest thing he had to family—except for his aunt, of course—but he wasn't about to put up with meddling from them.

He handed Regina into the SUV and then rounded the car to get into the driver's side.

They'd driven in silence for five minutes when Regina said, "Everything all right?"

He glanced at her, taking note of the concern in her eyes, the seriousness of her expression.

Damn. He must look like a mad bull loose on the streets of Pamploma.

He forced himself to relax. "Yeah. Everything's fine."

Liar.

Truth was, he was wound up tighter than a major-league pitcher who should have retired years ago.

He put it down to the ambiguity of the situation between him and Regina. So long as Johnson was at large, the criminal would hover over them both, a constant, unwanted presence.

The irony that Johnson was indirectly to credit for his being near her at all was not lost on him.

Neither was the possibility that the felon could be the thing that pulled them apart.

Regina's soft laugh drew his gaze back to her. "I can practically hear your teeth grinding from here."

He realized she was right: he was grinding his teeth.

He was surprised at his chuckle. More surprised at the tension that seemed to leach from his muscles at her noticing his state of mind and trying to ease it.

"Where are we going now?" she asked, looking through the window at the road in front of them.

He hadn't realized he was driving to his apartment until just then.

"My place. I thought I might make us something to eat. You hungry? Or would you rather go out?"

She seemed to consider his words. "I'd like to see your place. Yes, I'm hungry. I work 'out' all day, so I'd enjoy a homemade meal."

He couldn't seem to look away from her smile. But a warning horn from the driver behind him told him he'd better.

They both laughed.

And just like that, the awkwardness he'd experienced at the the Barracks slipped away. His mind turned to what he could pick up to make for her, wondered what she'd think of his place...and imagined what she'd look like lying bare against his sheets...

LINC'S PLACE WAS comfortable. In fact, it wasn't all that unlike hers, really—a one-bedroom apartment that held the bare necessities and not much else. Well, except for the mammoth flat-screen TV. Judging by his taste in magazines, and the parts of the newspaper that were left open, she guessed sports dominated much of his viewing.

She smiled to herself as she walked around, the aroma of chicken frying filling her senses.

She paused in the door to the bedroom. Hello. Okay, makes two things that were different: the TV and their beds.

She stared at the king-size mattresses and the dark sheets and spread that were tangled on top and her hand went to her throat. Of course, he was tall, his feet hanging over the end of her simple double bed whenever he slept over, so perhaps the larger size was necessary.

But all she could seem to think about were the naughty things they could do together there...

"You can go in if you want."

She felt Linc's words against the back of her neck more than heard them with her ears. She shivered, her nipples growing sensitive as they hardened against her bra cups.

"Um, is anything in danger of burning?" she found herself whispering.

He nudged her hair aside and lightly kissed the back

of her neck, her full-flush reaction anything but light. "Only me."

Regina instinctively leaned against him, her bottom against his front. She felt his arousal press into her lower back. Any thought of food vanished from her mind, leaving only a deep hunger for him.

He chuckled softly. "I have the feeling we're going to need the, um, energy, so maybe we should eat first…"

She hummed her response, her eyes fluttering closed as she enjoyed his warmth.

She felt his hands on her arms, caressing before bracing her, holding her upright as he stepped back away from her.

"Beer?"

She blinked her eyes open and turned to smile at him. "Share one with me?"

"Deal."

She preceded him into the kitchen, taking a seat at a small table that was set for two, including what looked like an emergency candle that had been fused to a small plate, the small flame flickering from their movements as they settled themselves.

"Fajitas." She appreciated the amount of work done in a short time. Warm flour tortillas were wrapped in foil. A skillet held strips of chicken breast, white onions and red peppers. Sliced tomatoes and fresh shredded cheese were in bowls. Then, of course, there was the salsa. Regina plucked a white corn chip from another bowl and dipped it.

"Careful," he warned.

Too late. She'd crunched on the chip and felt the heat

of the sauce before the word was all the way out of his mouth.

She coughed. He handed her a plain tortilla and nudged her water glass closer to her.

Thankfully she hadn't eaten much, so another chip, this time without sauce, was all it took to stop her eyes from watering.

She laughed. "Hot."

"How I like it." His gaze raked over her face, telling her that's not all he liked hot.

He opened a beer and poured half of it into her chilled mug and the other into his while she went about putting together her fajita.

"You cook like this often?" she asked.

"Every day." He slid a tortilla onto his plate. "When you're on assignment, you have little say in what you eat. So when I'm home, I make a point of cooking for myself."

"Like this?"

He shrugged. "More or less."

"I can't tell you how often I just bring home something from the diner."

"I would too, if I worked there. It's as close to home cooking as you can come outside of home. At least from what I had."

She watched as he expertly rolled the filled tortilla, his hands dark against the white, his fingers thick and long.

She had difficultly swallowing the bite in her mouth.

He squinted at her. "The salsa again?"

She shook her head and finally managed to get it down. "No. The cook."

His eyes smiled at her as he took a bite of his fajita.

There was something sexily elemental about watching him eat…especially since he seemed to feel the same way, his gaze fastened on her mouth as she chewed.

"Your friends seem nice," she said, taking a sip of beer.

"My friends are insane."

"Your friends are the family you choose."

He tilted his head. "I've never looked at it that way before."

A spot of salsa was left at the side of his mouth. She indicated where it was, but he missed it. So she leaned across, braced the heel of her hand against his wide jaw and rubbed it onto her thumb. She automatically stuck the digit into her mouth and sucked.

She didn't realize he'd stopped chewing until she caught his intense gaze. It was all she could do to swallow her own saliva just then.

"Screw food," he said quietly.

Within two moves, he'd moved the table's contents to the counter and then reached for her, easily hauling her across it so she sat on the edge, his mouth on hers before she could catch a breath.

Mmm… This was definitely better than anything from a skillet. And much, much hotter. She tasted beer and hot sauce on his tongue.

His hands grasped her hips and then slid under her shirt, cupping her breasts through her bra. Regina shivered at the feel of his thumbs rasping over her stiff tips through the thin satin then gasped when he stripped the shirt off along with her bra, replacing his thumb with his mouth.

Oh, yes. Much better than food...

Her skin tingled where his mouth made contact. And it wasn't just the normal tingling, either. She realized that the salsa he'd eaten was adding to the heated sensation. And upping her excitement level.

He popped the buttons on her jeans one by one. She braced herself with her hands and lifted her hips from the table as he stripped the denim from her. The kitchen lights were on but she didn't feel one iota self-conscious; the need burgeoning within her wouldn't allow room for anything else. There was only the growing urgency to feel him inside her.

But if she was hoping that was imminent, she was mistaken. Instead, he stripped off his T-shirt and jeans, presenting himself in all his toned and massive glory. Her gaze snagged on his solid erection and she fidgeted, only to be held to the table by a stilling hand on her stomach as he leaned down to press his mouth to first one hip, then the other even as he parted her thighs with his other hand.

Regina's heart beat a thick, uneven rhythm in her chest, the sound and her own ragged breathing filling her ears as he drew his tongue in a line from one hip to the other...and then dipped lower.

She caught her breath as his tongue ran the length of her shallow crevice and then his mouth fastened on her tight, sensitive nub.

The same heat that had infused his attention to her nipples crashed over her like a wave, a combination of his hot mouth and the chili powder from the food. She moaned deep in her throat and spread her thighs even farther, dropping her head back as she gave herself over to sheer sensation…

Hot…

Linc took in the sight of Regina spread across his kitchen table, every inch of her bare and beautiful, and experienced a need so extreme he suspected he could come just looking at her.

She leaned back against her arms, her hair tousled, her green eyes half-lidded, her luscious lips parted. He followed the line of her neck to her collarbone and then down to where the tips of her breasts glistened from his suckling them. Her stomach trembled, matching the chaos shaking his insides.

And she tasted as good as she looked…

After initially having to hold her down to prevent her from interrupting his plans, he was happy she surrendered to his desire to please her as she had him, laying herself open to him. He ran his tongue up her inner thigh and then used his thumbs to part her swollen flesh, giving him access to the pink, most delicate parts of her.

He gently caught her clit between his teeth, basking in her low moan as he pulled the hypersensitive bit into his mouth. Her trembling transformed into shivers as he dipped first one then two fingers into her dripping channel, twisting them and then withdrawing.

Her hips bucked as she achieved orgasm and he held her still again, continuing to sample her as she shuddered and shook, her soft moan wending around him so he nearly climaxed with her.

Before her last shudder hit, he lifted, sheathed himself and then positioned his erection between her thick folds. She wrapped her legs around his hips and lifted herself from the table, welcoming him inside her.

Linc locked his jaw, holding on to control with the thinnest of lines.

Until now, they'd had sex only in the dark, denying him a full view of her...of them. Now he was determined to use the light to take in his visual fill. Registering the passion in her eyes, he then shifted his gaze to where they were joined. He watched himself enter her, her flesh closing around him, her juices glistening on his hard shaft, and then withdrew only to slide in to the hilt.

"Yes..."

The word could have come from him, or her, or both as he held himself steady, warding off his crisis with every shred of strength he possessed.

But when she ground against him, there was no stopping off anything. He grasped her hips and stroked her hard and fast, racing toward a certain end so they might begin again...

16

THERE DIDN'T SEEM to be any surface, hard or soft, in Linc's apartment they didn't utilize during their sack session last night…and Regina was feeling it, in good ways and bad.

One of the bad was that it had to end. Dawn broke and so did their evening activities, sleep playing a very small role. Which was okay, she thought as he drove her back to her place. Since she had the day off from the diner and classes, she could catch up on some much-needed rest.

He'd offered to make breakfast that morning, but she'd insisted they make it together, the camaraderie between them warming her as he made eggs, she tended to bacon, and they both made and buttered toast and set the table.

Of course, the temptation to end the meal as she had the night before had loomed large…but ultimately they were both too spent to do anything more than smile suggestively at each other as they openly considered the option.

The time outside time had helped distract her from

her conversation yesterday with the hospital physician in charge of her mother's care; he'd told her he was keeping the older woman under for at least another forty-eight hours.

Linc pulled to the curb outside her apartment and shut off the engine. She smiled. "You want to come in for a cup of coffee?"

"Do you think that's a good idea?"

"Mmm...I always think it's a good idea."

His chuckle sent a shiver racing over her skin as he took the keys from the ignition and opened the door.

She followed suit, leading the way to her apartment. Halfway there, she again experienced that odd sensation of being watched. Her shiver turned to a shudder and she looked around, not seeing anything out of the ordinary as she unlocked her apartment door.

"Wait," Linc said quietly.

Regina's fingers froze on the handle. He reached for her hand, gently moving it away and tucking her behind him even as he drew his firearm. She swallowed thickly, watching as he swung the door open and led the way inside with his gun.

"Damn," she heard him say a moment later from somewhere inside.

She moved into the living room...and immediately saw what had prompted his response: her bedroom looked as if a flock of seagulls had nested there overnight and left their feathers behind.

Her feet slowly took her to the doorway. Everything had been torn apart: her pillows, the mattresses. Her clothes were strewn about, her closet had been ransacked. She absently wrapped her arms around herself, unable to believe her eyes.

"He did come back," she whispered to herself.

She turned to find Linc already on his cell phone, calling in the break-in.

"I...I don't understand," she said once he finished the call. "The original responding officers told me the chances the intruder would return were between slim to none."

Linc looked everywhere but at her. "Yes, well, this one ranks somewhere between them, I guess."

"What about the security equipment?"

"He bypassed them. Difficult, but not impossible."

"I don't get it. What would someone with those types of skills want with me?"

He met her gaze full-on. "You tell me."

LINC HATED TO TURN the tables on her, but the truth was, her stricken expression made him feel guiltier than he had in years.

Yes, he'd suspected Johnson would return last night. Worse, he had hoped he would return. But he'd counted on the silent alarm to alert him to the break-in so he could catch his no-good ass and send him back to prison.

That the son of a bitch had not only somehow disarmed the system, but tore up Regina's place again, made him angrier still.

Two hours later the report was filed, the place was cleaned up, new mattresses were on order and set to be delivered the next day. He decided to take Regina to Lazarus with him, his agenda not merely to keep her safe.

"You want me to what?"

"I want you to learn how to handle a firearm."

Her brows shot up as if she'd just finally registered his words. "I've never held a gun in my life."

"Yes, well, that's at least ten years too long in my estimation." He led her to the armory and considered the options before selecting a .44 Magnum. He turned to find her eyes larger than skeet disks. The expression on her beautiful face further served to endear her to him.

"Too big?" he asked.

"Way."

He chuckled and turned back toward the rack, choosing a .40 Smith & Wesson. She shook her head; he took her hand and placed the automatic in her palm, aiming the barrel toward the floor. "You'll get used to it," he said firmly.

He heard her swallow as she lifted the gun to examine it.

"First lesson is never hold a gun like that. Always handle it so the barrel is pointed at the ground unless you plan on shooting someone or something."

She nearly dropped the weapon in her hurry to do as he suggested. "It's loaded?"

"No, not yet. But you never know, so it's better to be safe than sorry."

She nodded and readjusted her grip. "It's heavy."

"Yes. It is. And it's designed to take care of some very heavy business."

She stared at him. "Do you really think I'll have to use it?"

"I really think it's a good idea you know how to, just in case it's necessary."

He showed her how to load the clip.

"Come on."

He led the way back to the corridor and to the right, then opened the door for her. She preceded him out, holding the gun out in front of her as if she might catch something.

"It won't bite you," he said with a chuckle.

"No, it's just capable of killing me."

He shook the box of ammo he picked up on the way out. "Not without these."

"Small comfort."

He led her to the open-firing range where two recruits were set up with ear protection and goggles. When they spotted him, they instantly stood upright and unloaded their firearms.

"Sir," they said almost in unison and then left the range.

Regina laughed. "Sir?"

Linc grimaced. He had no idea why the younger men treated him as if he was an officer. But he figured better that than a backslapping buddy.

"Hush and load your weapon."

She blinked at him and the ammo he held out.

"Go ahead."

He watched her pop the clip and the cartridge hit the ground. She gasped and he smiled, taking the gun from her as she retrieved the clip. She blew on it, making him smile wider.

She looked awkwardly at him and then the clip. He held his hand out and she gave it up. He placed the pistol on a nearby ledge and then reached for an oilcloth and properly cleaned the dirt off the clip, loaded the rounds one by one and then slid it home. She jumped. He handed the firearm back to her.

"Finger," he warned.

"Oh." She took her index finger off the trigger and placed it on the guard.

He turned her around and urged her toward the firing line. She began to lift the gun and he pressed her arms back down, placing headphones over her ears and protective glasses on her eyes, then put his own on.

She looked at him. He nodded. "Aim for the target straight on," he said.

She lifted the gun.

"Wait."

It had been so long since he'd worked with a greenhorn, he'd forgotten how much technique actually went into squeezing off a decent shot.

"Stand like this." He indicated where he had his feet squared, his body angled slightly to the right.

She did as he asked.

"Now, hold your right arm straight out. Yes, like that. It's got a kick, so you're going to take the impact with your shoulder. Brace it. That's right." He walked behind her, running his left hand up under her left arm. "Now, support your right hand and wrist with your left."

"Like this?"

"How's it feel?"

"How's it supposed to feel?"

He chuckled and remained where he was directly behind her.

"Okay, now I want you to squeeze the trigger, not pull it..."

"Now?"

"Whenever you're ready."

Long moments passed. He began to think she might not shoot at all. Then she did, and ended up flat up against him from the force of the kick.

"Wow," she said so quietly he nearly didn't hear her through the protective ear wear.

Damn. He should have gone with a less powerful alternative. She probably wouldn't want to shoot again.

"How'd I do?"

Linc blinked and looked at the target. "Well, I'll be damned... Nearly a perfect shot."

She took off her gear. "What?"

"I said you pretty near hit it straight through the bull's-eye."

Beginner's luck. A fluke. No one hit the bull's-eye first time out.

Hell, in this case, he guessed he was lucky her shot didn't ricochet off something and hit him between the eyes.

"How much you want to bet I can do it again?" she asked.

Linc threw back his head and laughed. "You know what the chances of that are?"

She cocked a brow. "Somewhere between slim to none?"

He didn't miss her reference to what the police had

told her the odds were of her getting broken into again so soon after the first time.

He motioned toward the target. "She's all yours."

He stepped back this time and crossed his arms over his chest, enjoying watching her as she put her headphones and glasses back on. She looked so damn sexy, it was all he could do to remember to watch her posture—which was dead-on—and concentrate on giving her pointers she might need.

Just beyond her, he caught sight of some of the guys looking on, one of them Jason Savage. But right that minute, Linc didn't care what others might make of his attention on this girl. He was too mesmerized by the girl herself.

She squeezed off a second shot, just slightly rocking backward. Then she surprised him by taking another.

Four rounds later, they both took off their gear and considered her handiwork.

Five of the seven were inside the inner rings; the other two just outside.

"Incredible…"

Her laugh was more of a sexy giggle. "I'm a natural." She blew on her nails and rubbed them against the front of her shirt.

Yes, she was definitely a natural…not only in shooting, but in stealing the air from his lungs and chasing away any sort of rational thought.

"Watch the barrel," he said.

She looked at where she'd lifted the now-empty gun, so it was pointing straight at him, and corrected herself.

Not that it mattered. She might as well have a gun

trained on him the way he was feeling. Hell, it would probably be a lot safer than the invisible one she aimed.

Jason came out. "Hey, Linc. Got a minute?"

He looked at his friend and partner then back at Regina. "You want to go again?" he asked.

"Love to!"

He pointed to the ammo behind them and then motioned for one of the professional trainers to join them. After introducing them, he told Regina he'd be nearby and then left her to annihilate a fresh target...

17

REGINA WAS EXHILARATED. Had she known shooting a gun would feel so empowering, she would have signed up for classes long ago. At the very least, she felt loads better than she had earlier after discovering her apartment had been broken into for a second time.

After the third go around, and equally accurate shots, she'd removed her gear and handed everything off to Dominic, the pro Linc had assigned to train her. He'd returned to her side then, looking glum.

"I have something I gotta do," he'd said.

She'd smiled at him. "What? Like work? Go figure."

"I don't feel comfortable leaving you alone. Do you want to stay here until I'm done? Or you could stay at my place…"

She'd reached out and touched the side of his handsome, worried face. "I was thinking maybe I'd go to work at the diner for a couple hours. Trudy called earlier and asked if I could fill in."

"Are you sure?" he'd asked.

"I'm sure." She shook out her hands and arms. "For some strange reason, I'm feeling great."

"Well, then, come on. I want to give you one of the guns."

Alarm bells went off then. "Whoa. Isn't that illegal? Don't I need a permit or something?"

"I won't tell if you don't. I'll feel better knowing you're armed."

"It's only a couple hours, right? And I'm just going to the diner. I should be fine until then."

Truthfully, she was touched by his attentiveness. But she didn't think she was anywhere near ready to carry a firearm on her own. Despite her good shooting today, she'd probably end up blowing a hole in her foot if the occasion ever called to use a weapon.

The idea sent shivers down her spine.

Linc had driven her home to retrieve her own car, and tried again to give her a firearm, but she'd refused. Now, four hours later, she'd put in a busy shift, her feet ached, but she was still smiling despite the events of the morning.

"You going home?" the diner owner asked, coming to stand next to her where she gathered her things from her locker.

"No. I'm going to a…friend's."

She'd filled Trudy and the others in on the break-ins and they were understandably concerned. Linc had waited for her at her apartment while she changed and insisted she pack an overnight bag and go directly to his place after her shift. He'd even given her a key.

The mere idea made her feel as she had earlier, when she'd squeezed the trigger of the .357.

"Yes, well, you know you can call me if you need anything."

Regina gave Trudy a quick hug. "Thank you."

She slung her bag over her shoulder and headed out through the dining room to the front door. She'd gotten there late and had to park halfway up the block. She fished her car keys out of her purse as she walked, noticing the sun had already set over the Rockies, leaving the sky a perfect blue since it wouldn't actually set for another hour.

She unlocked the car door, climbed in and started the ignition.

Something went around her neck from behind. "Drive, bitch."

LINC TEXTED REGINA an hour earlier to ask how her day was going even as he concentrated on finishing up an action plan in the main Lazarus conference room with Jason, Megan and Darius. The job was crucial. But no matter how important, he couldn't seem to take his mind off Regina.

She'd texted him back to say she was going to stop at the market to pick up something for dinner. Then she'd meet him at his place.

Meet him at his place.

When was the last time he'd given a woman his key? It shocked him to realize he never had. This was another first in a long line of like firsts when it came to Regina Dodson.

Jason sidled up to him while Meg and Dari discussed a separate item.

"Hey, I think we can get the rest from here, you know, if you need to get out of here."

Linc glanced at him. Who'd have thought, after everything, that his friend could be so intuitive? Oh, on the battlefield, sure; there was nobody better to have by his side. But on the personal front, Jason was known to be a little more selfish.

"You discuss that matter with anyone else yet?" Linc asked him, referring to the Baltimore office.

Jason averted his gaze and shook his head. "It'll happen when it's meant to."

"What will?" Megan asked, automatically homing in on their conversation.

Linc stood up to his full height. "I've got to run. We good?"

Jason stared at him. Linc smiled back. "Fine. Throw a friend under the bus."

"I'm trying to keep you from getting hit by it," Linc said, clapping Jason on the shoulder.

All four of them paused.

While he was often the recipient of such gestures, this was the first time he'd ever made one himself.

"Yeah, well, you know where I am if you need me," Linc continued after clearing his throat.

"And that is?" Megan asked.

"On the other end of my cell phone."

Laughter and groans followed him from the room.

OH, GOD, OH, GOD, OH, GOD…

Regina was incapable of registering more than those words…and the fact that somehow, someway, her worst nightmare had just manifested itself into full-blown reality.

Her heart bruised her rib cage as she saw Billy Johnson reflected in her rearview mirror.

"Drive," he ordered again, returning her stare. He removed his hand from around her neck and then showed her a gun not unlike the one she'd handled earlier. A gun she might have even now, had she not refused to take it.

"Billy," she whispered, her throat raw from where he'd held it too tightly. "What? How?"

His chuckle was nothing like Linc's, low, rumbling. "Bet I'm the last person you expected to see, ain't I?"

She nodded, nearly hitting an oncoming car when she accidentally veered across the middle line.

"Pay attention to where you're going!"

It was somehow surreal to think she'd spent a year and a half obsessed with thoughts of what might happen if this moment ever occurred. But over the past couple of weeks, he'd barely entered her thoughts at all.

And now he was here…

"Wh-wh-where are we going?" she asked.

He sat back, grinning at her. "Just drive for now. I've dreamed about this moment forever. I intend to enjoy myself."

She shuddered from head to toe.

"I thought I'd never get you alone."

She squinted at him, dividing her attention between the road in front of her and the ghost behind her. What was he doing out of prison? How had he found her?

An image of her mother lying in an induced coma in a Maine hospital room loomed large in her mind.

Oh, God, oh, God, oh, God…

"What I really want to know right now is what in the hell are you doing with him?"

She stared at him through the rearview mirror, dumbfounded.

There was no doubt to whom he was referring. But the way he asked the question, with such venom, made her think it was more than just a casual inquiry.

A horn beeped behind her.

"Watch the goddamn road!" Billy leaned forward, resting his forearm on the seat rest. "And slow down. I don't want you to die before I have a chance to kill you."

Regina's lungs refused air as he caressed her hair with his revolver. She could smell the gun oil as clearly as she had earlier at the firing range. And he was holding his finger on the trigger, not on the guard.

"Tell me, Reggie, is he getting some of that sweet ass of yours?" He chuckled hideously. "What am I talking about? You two are sleeping at each other's places—of course he's screwing you." He leaned closer, whispering into her ear. "Does he turn you inside out? Does he do you like you know I can?"

The half a tuna sandwich she'd eaten for dinner threatened to rush up her throat. She swallowed hard to keep it down.

How long had he been watching her? And why?

Then her blood ran cold. He was the one who'd broken into her apartment.

Worse, she knew exactly why.

Billy continued, "Actually, I'm thinking maybe you could use a reminder of how good we used to be together. It hadn't entered my mind before, but now that I'm seeing you up close, I'm remembering just how sweet that ass of yours is…"

Regina jerked the steering wheel to the left, accidentally putting her directly in the stream of oncoming traffic.

Horns honked, tires squealed and Billy slid down his seat.

Her only intention had been to force his foul breath and even fouler words away from her, but an idea started to take root.

"Stupid move," he ground out, taking his spot behind her again as she righted the car. "I could have shot you."

She wanted to ask him why he hadn't. Why didn't he just pull the trigger and get it over with? But she was afraid her goading might compel him to do it. And while a short time ago she might have risked anything to escape, now…

Well, now she had Linc.

The thought didn't so much surprise her as give her hope. Her days were so much brighter with him in them. He reminded her what it was like to be alive. Vibrantly, thankfully, utterly alive.

Billy leaned closer to her again. She winced and pulled away, her fingers slick on the steering wheel. "How does it feel to be screwing the man who put me behind bars?"

Her lungs refused air.

What?

She tried to process what he was saying.

Linc…

"What?" she whispered.

"Oh, you didn't know?" Billy's laugh was self-satisfied, smug. "I'll be damned. I'd thought he'd told you about my breakout."

Regina barely heard him over the loud thud of her heartbeat.

"You don't think his being with you is a coincidence, do you? The girlfriend of the man he put away?"

"Ex," she said automatically, but it was said so softly she wondered if he'd heard her.

"FBI Special Agent Lincoln Carver Williams was the man who tracked me down in Maine and put me in jail." A metallic click made her cringe. She looked in the mirror to find him cocking his gun. "And after I'm done with you, I intend to put him in a box of an entirely different kind."

Her racing mind tried to process the details. She'd known Linc was an ex-Marine, but he hadn't said he'd also been with the FBI.

"Where's the money, Regina?"

The question forced her thoughts to the here and now although her heart was full of the pain Linc's betrayal had wrought.

"What money?"

He pressed the barrel of the gun against the side of her head. She briefly closed her eyes and said a prayer.

"Don't play with me, sweetheart. You know what money. I was the one who gave you the key to my place, remember?"

She remembered all too clearly.

"I don't have it," she told him.

"Not on you, no. Not anywhere at your place, either. But you have it somewhere."

Regina knew a moment of panic. What would he do if he knew she didn't have the money?

No, she didn't have to wonder, she knew. He'd kill her.

She eyed the gun in the rearview mirror along with the madman wielding it. She may not have a traditional weapon, but she was driving a hell of a large vehicle capable of doing damage.

"And right now, you're going to drive me to where you're hiding it. Aren't you, baby?"

He stroked the side of her face with the gun.

Quickly considering all the likely consequences, Regina decided on a course of action. She jerked the steering wheel to the left and stepped on the accelerator, zooming through a hole in oncoming traffic and passing over onto the curb. As she'd hoped, Billy slid across the seat and against the opposite door. As soon as she screeched to a halt, she got out of the car and made a run for it...

18

LINC'S ADRENALINE LEVEL shot through the roof as he rushed inside the Colorado Springs Police Operations Center. When he'd checked his cell locator and saw Regina was there, he'd raced to the station, his mind filled with anxiety.

He took in the open area with one glance and then headed for a familiar desk sergeant.

"Dodson, Regina. Where is she?"

Bruce blinked at him. "Hey, Linc. You look like you just ran a marathon. What's up?"

Linc was a familiar face around the precinct because of Lazarus. He'd made a point of introducing himself in the beginning, and then business had brought him in occasional contact with precinct personnel.

But right now, he suppressed the desire to grab a man he'd always seen as a friendly by the shirtfront. "A client is here. Regina Dodson. Where is she?"

Bruce frowned, apparently picking up on his impatience. "Oh, you must be talking about that attempted kidnapping case…"

Linc's ears started ringing and his mind filled with a string of curse words. Attempted kidnapping?

Good God in heaven, what had happened in the short time span he'd been otherwise occupied?

Johnson. He had no doubt.

"She's in the back with Jensen."

Linc rounded the desk and headed for the office of the lead detective.

"Hey, you can't just—"

He gave the guy a warning glance. The round man held up his hands even as he reached for the radio transmitter hanging on his front shirt pocket presumably to call for backup. But Linc reached the small, enclosed office before the desk sergeant could get out his first word.

He froze just inside the door. Regina was sitting huddled in one of the two visitors' chairs, by herself in the room. Relief rushed through him at seeing her safe.

Then she looked up at him and he felt as if he'd just stepped on an IED.

She knows...

The detective came up from behind him.

"Hey, Williams, what are you doing in here?"

"I know the lady."

The man glanced at Regina and then back at Linc.

"Funny," she said quietly. "I'm not sure I know you at all..."

DETECTIVE DAN JENSEN asked Linc to go to the public waiting area and he did so reluctantly. He wanted—no, needed—to talk to Regina now. Find out what happened. Make sure she was okay.

Beg her forgiveness.

He paced back and forth and forth and back in the front room, wishing he was anywhere else but there in that one moment. He didn't mean physically, although he would prefer not to be standing in a police station. Rather, he didn't like the situation he was in—keeping Regina in the dark as to his true intentions from the onset.

And as a result of his silence, she'd suffered at Johnson's hands.

"Whoa, buddy," the desk sergeant said. "You look two spits away from a full brawl."

Linc stared at him.

"Make that one."

He stared at his watch and then craned his neck to try to see down the hall where the detective's office was located. It had been a half hour since he'd been ousted. What could they be talking about?

The detective came out and handed a file to a nearby clerk.

Linc caught his eye. Dan frowned and came over to the front desk.

"Are you going to be done soon?" Linc asked.

"We finished about ten minutes ago. Miss Dodson requested to go out the back way. One of my guys took her home."

Damn, damn, damn!

He stormed from the precinct.

REGINA SAT IN THE MIDDLE of her couch, lights off, her arms wrapped around her knees, rocking back and forth.

Her throat felt raw, her nerves frayed and her heart as if it had been turned inside out.

How could Linc have lied to her?

Considering all that had happened in the past couple of hours, she found it surprising that's what hurt the most. It helped that a squad car was parked at the curb, watching the apartment. But she didn't think a lone cop would be much of a deterrent to Billy, should he decide to come after her again. And she was sure he would.

Still, not even fear of her ex could squash the pain she felt at Linc's betrayal.

He'd known. He'd known Billy had escaped from prison. Known he'd come after her. And he'd never said a word.

She discovered she was shivering and pulled a throw from the side of the sofa to cover her knees. Her new mattresses wouldn't be delivered until tomorrow, which meant she'd be spending the night there anyway. That is, if she managed to get any sleep at all. A prospect she found highly doubtful. How was she supposed to sleep when there was a madman after her, bent on taking a long-nurtured revenge? And when the man she was falling in love with had hurt her more deeply than her ex?

A hot teardrop rolled over the side of her nose and onto her hand where her check rested against it, followed by another.

She recalled every moment since the time their gazes first met at the club. The smiles…the hot kisses…the soft moans…his strong arms around her making her feel sexy and safe.

A knock at the door caused her to jump.

"Regina? It's Linc."

She slowly lifted her head to stare at the closed and locked barrier, taking in the red-and-green glowing lights connected to the security system he'd installed. She knew all he had to do was use his key and bypass everything.

Another knock.

"I really don't want to have this conversation through the door," he said.

She sat for long moments, as if caught in some sort of strange time warp. She hurt, she was numb and when she moved it appeared to be in slow motion.

Finally, she managed to rise from the sofa and walk to the door. Her heart pounding in her chest, she opened it a crack and held out her hand palm up.

"Look at me," he said.

She bit hard on her bottom lip and shook her head.

The *beep beep* of the countdown on the security system sounded.

He placed his copy of her house key in her hand.

"Is that the only one?" she asked.

"It's the only one."

She quietly closed the door and the automatic lock slid home.

LINC RAISED HIS HAND to knock again...but instead brought it to rest softly against the door, the metal cold against his palm. The pain on her beautiful face, the telltale signs she'd been crying, ripped him to shreds.

Knowing he was responsible shredded his soul again.

"Just so you know," he said through the door. "I'm going to stay out here all night."

No response. Not that he expected one. Hell, he'd be lucky if she didn't call in his unwanted presence to the squad car parked at the curb and have his sorry ass carted off.

He leaned back against the wall next to the door and crossed his arms. There was no way he was going to leave her alone with that son of a bitch on the loose somewhere.

On the drive over, he'd picked up the details via phone on the attempted kidnapping. It was an easy task considering the abductor was an escaped convict who'd crossed state lines, which made it a government matter, more specifically the U.S. Marshals office. His FBI contact easily obtained the information and relayed it quickly.

He checked his cell again, hoping for a follow-up call outlining stolen cars, possible sightings and reports of robberies within a fifty-mile radius that fit Johnson's M.O. Something, anything that might afford him a clue as to the bastard's whereabouts.

Damn. He should have been paying closer attention. He should have known Johnson would do what he had. Instead, Linc been so distracted, he'd barely been able to concentrate on anything other than needing to be near the woman inside the apartment for reasons that had nothing to do with protecting her…yet everything to do with it.

"Have you eaten?"

He was surprised by the words said through the door. He suppressed the desire to ask her to repeat the question for fear she wouldn't. Then he cleared his throat and answered honestly. "No."

Linc leaned his head back against the wall and took a deep, fortifying breath. When the door opened a few minutes later, he quickly stood upright to face her. But she still refused to meet his gaze.

She looked a little better. She'd apparently washed her face and pulled her hair back, making her look years younger than she was.

She held out a plate containing a sandwich. He took it.

"Thanks," he said.

She nodded and began to close the door again.

"Regina, wait."

The door stopped a few inches shy of home, but he could no longer see her.

"I just wanted to say… I mean, all of this was never… It's important that you know…"

For a man renowned for getting to the point, he seemed to be having a hard time of it now.

He cleared his throat. "I'm sorry."

No response, and then the door softly closed again.

Damn.

Damn, damn, damn, damn, damn.

He considered the sandwich in his hands and then the door. Just then, he'd have had trouble eating lobster, his appetite was so low. But if it killed him, he was going to eat this. Solely because Regina had made it for him. And the fact that she had was evidence that she might be able, at some point, to forgive him…

19

IT WAS THREE o'clock in the morning and Regina still sat in the dark on the sofa, unable to sleep, unable to shut her mind down, unable to forget the fact that Linc stood outside her door like a stubborn oak, refusing to leave.

She got up, looked out the window at where a new squad car sat. The police had changed shifts around midnight. Then she stepped to the door where a glance through the peephole told her Linc was still there, only part of his left arm where it was apparently folded over his chest visible.

Disarming the alarm, she kept on the chain and then cracked open the door. He immediately filled the space with his tall, handsome frame.

"Everything okay?" he asked.

Everything was far from okay, but she knew that wasn't what he meant, so she told him it was.

She slid to sit on the floor by the door and then leaned her back against the wall directly across from where he had been leaning on the other side. "Talk to me."

She wasn't sure what she wanted him to say. He'd

already apologized. Although she wasn't entirely clear what it had covered. Was he sorry he'd been caught in the lie? Sorry he hadn't been able to stop Billy?

Sorry for getting involved with her?

"Thanks for the sandwich."

She tucked her chin into her chest, finding it impossible to believe he'd made her smile.

"You're welcome."

Silence.

Which was okay with her. She felt better just knowing he was mere inches away. And she could hear him move as he presumably sat down too.

"I am sorry," he said quietly.

She found it difficult to swallow, the hollow air around her heart expanding.

"Regina?"

"What?" she whispered.

"Do you forgive me?"

She considered her response for a moment. "I don't know."

She heard him shift again.

"I can understand that, I guess," he said.

She heard a car drive past on the street, somewhere a dog barked.

"It might be easier if I knew what you were apologizing for," she said so quietly she wasn't sure if he heard her.

"Where do I begin…?"

She fought the urge to say "the beginning's always a good place," and instead rested her head against the wall and closed her eyes, waiting for him to continue.

"That night, at the club, I never expected your friend to approach me…"

She half smiled at the memory as well as the fact that he was starting at the beginning.

"I intended to ignore her. But then I saw you."

She swallowed hard. "But you already knew who I was?"

She heard him take a deep breath. "At that point, I'd been following you for two days."

She leaned over and peered through the crack, catching sight of his handsome profile.

"I never expected to go home with you," he said. "And after that first night, I never expected there to be a second."

"But you were still watching me…"

A pause. "I was still watching you."

Silence settled between them and she rested against the wall again.

"Is it true?" she asked. "That you originally apprehended Billy?"

He shifted again. "Yes."

"Did you know about me back then?"

"No. I mean, I knew what was in his file, but there was no picture. Only the basic information. Name, D.O.B., parents' names…"

She winced.

"I never had to go beyond that because I caught up with him before the next step was necessary…"

She considered that. "When did Billy escape?"

He told her.

She recalled the sensation of being watched, of something being wrong. But was that a result of Billy's prison break? Or of Linc's tailing her, hoping to catch Billy?

"Why didn't you tell me, once we became...familiar?"

"I couldn't."

"Because you were afraid I'd be upset?"

"Because I was afraid you'd stop looking at me the way you did."

The sweet words seemed to have double the impact coming from such a big, rough-and-tumble guy.

"I know, it sounds corny..."

She reached around the door and placed her hand on his arm. "No, it doesn't sound that way at all."

He placed his other hand over hers, holding it there.

"Regina...can I come in? Please?"

She sat without saying anything for a long moment.

"My ass is starting to hurt."

She laughed. Then she slid her hand from under his and moved away from the door. A moment later, she held out a throw pillow to him.

"Not exactly what I had in mind," he said, accepting it.

"It's all you're getting." For now.

She didn't say the words, but she might as well have.

Truth was, she knew Linc was as sincere as they came. She may have questioned her judgment when it came to men and relationships once. Solely based on her experiences with Billy.

But now, she had something to compare him against.

And was coming to understand that though she'd always held out hope Billy would change, she'd always seen him for who he really was.

And she had seen and was seeing Linc for who he was. There was no need to change him.

Well, mostly.

"Did…keeping me in the dark bother you?" she asked.

"Tied me up in knots. Especially when I got news Johnson was circling closer and…"

"And I was placed in harm's way."

He took a deep breath. "Yes." A pause. "Only it wasn't supposed to happen that way. I was supposed to be there to protect you."

Now that she was dealing with the pain inflicted by his deception, the day's earlier events crashed back on her like a violent gust of wind. Her hand went to her neck, feeling Billy's fingers there all over again. Hearing his hateful words ringing in her ears. Smelling the stench of his breath…

He could have killed her without batting an eye. And in the absence of an adrenaline rush, or the fight-or-flight instinct that went with it, her blood ran cold.

Had she really loved him once? It seemed impossible to believe given present circumstances. She supposed her mother had been right when she'd said living in a small town had limited Regina's options. She needed to see what else was out there.

And finally she had. Which threw everything else into stark relief.

She shivered.

"Cold?" Linc asked.

She blinked to find him peering in at her. "It's still ninety degrees out."

"I'm guessing you still may be suffering the effects of shock."

She nodded. "Probably."

Then a thought occurred to her. She pushed away from the wall and knelt to face the crack and him.

"How did you know he'd come for me?" she asked.

He began to disappear, presumably to lean back against the wall out of sight.

"Don't. Face me and tell me."

He hesitated and then honored the first part of her request, although he appeared to have trouble with the second.

"At this point, I can't imagine what you'd be afraid to say."

She watched him grimace in the dim light from an outdoor wall sconce. "The missing money."

Regina's breathing slowed. She'd guessed what his answer might be—she just hadn't worked out how she'd respond to it.

"He told his cellmate you had his cash and he was coming after you to get it."

She looked down at where she worried her hands in her lap.

She vividly recalled her prison visit to Billy. His asking her to close up his apartment, give his things to his father...but to keep something for him. Since calls and visits were monitored, he hadn't specified what the "something" was. He'd said she'd know what it was when she came across it.

She had never anticipated it would be a bag full of

cash, presumably from the bank robbery that had placed him behind bars.

"Do you think I have it?" she asked Linc quietly.

She felt his gaze on her face and blinked up to meet it.

"The money. Do you think I'm in possession of it?"

"That's not important. What is, is that Johnson thinks you are."

Not the answer she was looking for.

She shifted until she was leaning against the wall again, falling silent.

"Regina?"

She didn't answer.

And she didn't know if she would...

LINC LIGHTLY KNOCKED the back of his head against the hard brick of the wall. An internal alarm bell went off the instant he'd responded, telling him "wrong answer."

He had answered honestly enough. It *wasn't* important. She hadn't been charged or convicted of a crime. Billy Johnson had.

But her sudden silence told him it wasn't the answer she was looking for.

He recrossed his arms over his chest. While he was glad she hadn't closed the door or moved away from it, whatever headway he'd hoped they'd made in the last little while was slipping away.

At this rate, he was never going to get back into her apartment.

His cell phone vibrated. He took it out and read the screen.

Damn.

This was the absolute worst time for him to be leaving. But if he held out any hope of this thing with Johnson ending anytime soon, he had to.

"Regina?" he said again.

She didn't answer.

"I'm going to get a couple of Lazarus guys to watch after you. I'll let the local uniforms know."

He got to his feet, surprised when he found she had opened the door.

"Are you leaving?"

He nodded. "I've got a line on Johnson. I'm going to check it out." He looked over his shoulder at the squad car. "My guys will be here in less than a half hour. Until then…"

He took his own .357 out of his hip holster.

"It works just like the one you used today. Just point and shoot."

She appeared hesitant.

He reached out and took her right hand and then placed the weapon in it.

"Don't argue. If you'd taken the one I offered earlier…"

He didn't finish the thought. He didn't have to. He could tell by her grimace her thoughts were venturing in the same direction.

"Ground," he reminded her.

She automatically pointed the barrel downward.

"I have little doubt you'll hit whatever you take aim at."

He watched a swallow work down her elegant throat. He found himself wishing he could follow the movement with his lips against her skin…and prayed she'd trust him enough to allow him the privilege again.

"If you need anything…"

"Police are watching the place."

He nodded. "Still."

"I have your number."

He squinted at her. "Wish you would have called me earlier."

She offered up a ghost of a smile. "Trust me, you wouldn't have liked what I would have called you."

He chuckled. "No, I probably wouldn't have." He reached out and touched the side of her face. "But I would have deserved it."

She turned her head away and he let her. What other choice did he have?

"All right, then…"

"All right."

"Good night." It seemed like a stupid thing to say; he doubted "good" would factor anywhere into the equation.

"Good night," she returned quietly.

He forced his feet to carry him away, listening as she closed the door and rearmed the alarm system.

20

LINC PULLED TWO of Lazarus's best men from other jobs to cover Regina, even as he holed up inside his office tracking Johnson's possible movements on a map he'd tacked to a large corkboard he'd liberated from a nearby conference room. Three hours had passed since he'd left Regina's apartment, but it felt like ten. He checked his cell phone again; she hadn't called. And he wouldn't call her. Not because he was afraid she might not answer, but because he didn't want to chance waking her in case she'd managed to get some sleep.

She was safe. For now. But he was brainstorming methods to keep her that way at the same time as he plotted ways to finally catch the man responsible for her needing protection.

He couldn't keep her locked up inside her apartment for the duration. Sending her to stay with her friend Vivienne probably wasn't a viable option, either. Nor was her going to his place. It was safe to assume Johnson had been watching her and knew not only where he lived, but Vivienne, as well. He likely had Regina's regular routine memorized, which meant Linc had to think a step ahead in order to stay that way.

The telephone extension rang on the table in the middle of the room; he punched the speaker button. "What you got?"

"Convenience-store holdup. Single male fitting Johnson's M.O. Ten miles outside C.C."

Linc pushed a tack into the board. He'd pulled in two additional guys to work with him and had even called Jason, who had immediately come in, no questions asked.

Well, until now anyway.

He tried to ignore where Jason leaned against the door. Up until now he'd been following up on leads in his own office across the hall. Linc wished he would go back to it.

"Tell me who this Johnson guy is again?"

Linc asked the caller to contact him with anything else then stabbed the button to disconnect. He stared at his friend briefly before turning away.

Jason stepped inside and joined Linc next to the board. "Details, I know. What I want to know is what is he to you?"

"He's worth nearly a quarter of a mil in reward money to Lazarus."

His friend rubbed his chin, causing a rasping sound since he was in need of a shave. "Official business, then? Is that your stance? Are we expanding our operations to include fugitive recovery?"

Linc ignored him.

"He wouldn't have anything to do with the girl you brought to the Barracks the other night, would he?"

Linc's muscles tightened, but he tried to shake it off.

"You know, the pretty one you nearly decked me over?"

"Watch your step, Savage."

Jason chuckled. "Okay, so it is. What is she to Johnson? Ex-girlfriend?"

Linc took a deep breath. Obviously, Jason wasn't going to stop until he either got some answers or Linc did deck him but good. "Yes."

"And the reason we're working in the middle of the night instead of waiting until morning…?"

"He tried to abduct her yesterday."

"I see. Good reason."

"Did you expect otherwise?"

Jason shrugged. "No. I just wanted verbal verification, is all."

"Yeah, well, you know what they say about curiosity."

"That the prosecutor used it against the cat?"

"No, it killed it."

"Ah, yes, that." Jason grinned at him. "Guess I'd better get back to work, then."

"Guess you'd better."

His friend started walking toward the door. "I think the words you're looking for here are 'thank you.'"

Linc turned toward him. "You're welcome."

Jason laughed and he grinned.

"No, those would be my words. Only I haven't decided yet if they're what I'd say to a guy in love who woke me up in the middle of the night to work his girlfriend's case."

In love…girlfriend…

The words zoomed around Linc's head long after Jason ducked out of the office to return to his own.

Was his friend right? Could this have waited until morning?

While he might be working at full capacity now, in a couple of hours lack of sleep would begin to kick in, limiting his ability to function. Would his actions end up complicating the situation instead of simplifying it?

And what happened when the other partners arrived in a few hours to find them still working? If he thought Jason's questions invasive, he was sure to get even more.

Damn.

He drew in a deep breath and then slowly let it out, looking for a pattern on the map in front of him.

THE MERE ARRIVAL of dawn brought with it a measure of normalcy Regina had been terrified she might never experience again. She'd nodded off a couple of times only to awaken a few minutes later convinced she'd heard a sound.

It was just after eight and she poured herself a second cup of coffee while she checked her cell phone again. No calls, no texts. She pushed her hair, which was damp from a shower, back from her face and went to the table to continue studying.

Correction: continue trying to study. As it was, she'd read the same passage at least four times and hadn't retained a word.

She sipped her coffee and turned the page of the

textbook only to turn it back again. She'd already called the Maine hospital to check on her mother's status. Folded the blanket and put it and the pillow she'd had on the sofa away and straightened up. Since she'd thoroughly cleaned after both break-ins, she didn't need to do that. She'd spoken to Trudy at the diner last night. The woman had told her to let her know if she needed anything and to take as much time as she needed.

Maybe getting dressed would help. The furniture store had scheduled delivery of her new mattresses from nine to eleven, so it might be a good idea to be wearing more than a robe when they arrived.

She found herself absently stroking the front of the apparel in question, her mind drifting back to Linc, as it seemed to have a tendency to do a lot lately.

She propped her elbow on the table and rested her chin in her palm, thinking about how he had sat outside her door the night before. Talked to her. Apologized. Touched her face when he explained he had to leave.

She recalled his avoidance when she'd asked if he thought she had the money from the bank robbery.

She picked up her cell phone again and stared at the blank screen.

"Oh, just call him and get it over with already," she whispered.

But she couldn't.

So much had happened. Not merely over the past day, but the past week.

After Billy...well, she'd never really seen herself falling for anyone else again. Her mother always spoke of once-in-a-lifetime love and for her it had been Regina's father. Regina had always believed she'd wasted her shot on Billy. That the love she had given him, however ill-fated, was it. She'd never be able to love again with that kind of unfettered fullness.

Then came Linc...

Her heart gave that gentle lurch that always accompanied thoughts of him, now with a dull ache. To think, all along he had known her as Billy's ex. That, in fact, Billy had been the sole reason he'd been interested in her at all.

She swallowed hard. That wasn't entirely true. Still, considering what had gone on between them over the past week, reviewing conversations, she cringed. She'd believed they'd been starting from ground level and had shared things with him she'd never told anyone else. Things about her and Billy that had been intimate and personal. And he'd not only listened, he'd asked questions.

Had he been pumping her for information? Had he thought she was in touch with Billy? Did he believe she'd known Billy had escaped from prison and was secretly helping him?

She tightly closed her eyes against the sudden onslaught of stinging tears.

The chirping of her cell phone startled her. She quickly wiped her eyes with the end of her robe sleeve as if the caller would be able to see her and answered without looking at the display.

"Regina?"

Linc.

Tears flooded her eyes all over again.

"Hey," she said weakly.

There was a long pause. "You okay?"

To her horror, she sniffled. "I'm...fine."

"You don't sound fine."

That's because she wasn't. "Is there something you wanted?"

She could almost see his wince and regretted her curt question. Still, she bit on her bottom lip to keep from apologizing for it.

"One of my guys, Dominic Falzone, is going to be coming to your door with the furniture deliverymen in a few minutes. He's going to check for listening and tracking devices."

She frowned and looked around, seeing her place in a new, unflattering light. "You think something's here?"

"I'm thinking there might be. If there is, Dominic will find it."

She sniffled again. "Okay. Can you ask him to give me a few minutes?"

"Sure."

"Linc?"

She had no idea what she wanted to say, only that she wanted to keep him on the phone awhile longer.

"Yes?" he prompted.

"Um...thanks."

"Sure."

She swore she could hear the smile in his voice. And was surprised she wanted to smile in return.

She hurried to the other room to change and was just tying her hair back when a knock sounded at the door. She went to open it.

A nice-looking young man dressed in nondescript clothing and carrying a clipboard introduced himself and she motioned him in. Behind him were the deliverymen bringing in her mattresses.

After directing the delivery guys to her bedroom, she turned to Dominic: "Linc said you'd be stopping in. Please, do what you have to."

"Thanks, ma'am. This shouldn't take long."

Had he just called her "ma'am"? Yes, she realized with a start, he had. Didn't he know her mother was a ma'am? That she was still a miss?

But she wasn't about to argue with him. Instead, she offered him a coffee, which he politely refused, then returned to the kitchen, telling him to let her know if he needed anything.

Ten minutes later the deliverymen had gone and Dominic came into the kitchen. Regina stopped where she was reading her textbook and watched Dominic sweep the countertop and cupboards with what looked like a small metal detector.

"Anything?" she asked.

"No, not yet, ma'am."

She grimaced. What was he, a whole two years younger than her? He was going to have to stop with the ma'am.

She opened her mouth to say the same when the device made a sound as he moved it over the table she sat at.

"Oh."

They both stared at the table's contents. Her purse, her course materials and her coffee.

"Do you mind?" he asked, lifting her purse.

"No, no. Go ahead."

He moved it to the counter and waved the device over it. Nothing.

He returned to the table and removed the items one by one, all with the same result.

The only remaining item was the book she was reading.

Since it was the only thing on the table, he didn't bother to remove it. Instead, he verified it was the source of the beeping. Then he shut off the device and moved the book closer. He leafed through the pages, turned it upside down and shook it, and then opened the back cover, running his fingers over the inside. He did the same with the front.

His gaze met hers as he peeled back the paper lining the hardback, revealing an insect-looking device.

Regina wrapped her arms around herself. "What is it?"

"Run-of-the-mill tracking device, ma'am."

She barely registered the ma'am as she tried to wrap her mind around what exactly this all meant...

21

"NO, LEAVE IT THERE," Linc told Dominic when he called with the news. "We want him to believe nothing's changed."

He'd suspected Johnson had bugged Regina. Considering the guy had bypassed the security system with ease, Linc had been afraid at how high tech the bugging might be. He was relieved to discover it was as basic as they came and that Johnson probably had gained access to Regina's textbook via her car where she usually left her class materials, rather than through another channel.

He told Dominic to resume his post and ended the call, dialing Regina directly thereafter.

"Hey," he said. "You okay?"

She spoke to someone who was presumably Dominic and then he heard her rearm the alarm system. "I'm beginning to wonder if I'll ever be okay again."

He didn't know what to say, so he said nothing.

"It feels…funny to just leave the tracking device there."

"I know. But it's important he thinks nothing's changed."

"But everything has changed."

She didn't have to tell him that. If he could turn back the hands of time…

He'd do what, exactly?

He'd never been one to indulge in self-defeating behavior. Curious he was doing it now.

"So what should I do?" she asked.

"How do you mean?"

"I'll go stir crazy if I stay in the apartment all day."

"What do you want to do?"

"Resume my life."

Linc paced across his office and back, the cell held tightly to his ear, suppressing the desire to ask whether or not he'd be included in that. "I can't let you do that just yet."

"You can't let me?"

He grimaced. "I don't think it's a good idea if you do."

"Better."

He felt the urge to smile.

"I'm thinking about going in to work."

Last night, he'd had her car picked up from the towing yard, had it checked over by his guys and then returned it to her place. So she had the freedom to go anywhere she wanted.

"Okay," he said.

"Okay?"

"May I suggest you call Dominic to let him know what you're doing?"

Silence.

"Here's his number." He recited it to her.

"Okay," she said. "When will I see you?"

Hearing the wistfulness in her voice, he wanted to tell her in five minutes, but he had a couple of solid leads he was about to go out and follow up.

Besides, he didn't think it was a good idea that Johnson spot him anywhere near Regina. Last night he'd made a mistake in judgment by camping out on her doorstep. But he hoped it ended up working out to his advantage. If Johnson had been watching, he'd surely understood that Regina was upset with him. By keeping his distance, perhaps Johnson would let his guard down and his men could step in and grab him.

But he fully intended to find him first…

"I don't know," he answered honestly.

A long pause. He imagined her worrying her bottom lip in that sexy way she had and suppressed a groan.

"Okay," she said.

Damn, he was coming to hate that word. Especially since the current usage meant anything but okay.

"I guess I'll talk to you later, then," she said.

He agreed and the call was over.

Linc let the phone drop to his side and stood for a long moment, allowing emotion to sweep through him.

"Ready, champ?" Jason said from the door, holstering his Glock and then sliding a vest on over it.

"Born ready."

THAT UNSETTLING SENSATION she was being watched followed Regina everywhere. As Linc had requested, she called Dominic to let him know her plans, and then informed the uniform officer sitting at the curb of same, although he'd shared there were no plans to follow her and he had no idea if another car would be posted there that night.

She'd put in a full lunch shift, and even managed at one busy point to forget about the past twenty-four hours. But always there, in the back of her mind, clinging to her like a stench she couldn't rid herself of, was the memory of Billy emerging from the shadows of the backseat and putting his hands around her neck.

She shuddered as she removed her apron, folded it and hung it in her locker. She sat down on the bench, feeling gratefully tired, but wondering what she was supposed to do with the rest of her day.

Her cell phone vibrated in her skirt pocket. She slid it out, her heart skipping a beat as she saw Linc's name.

"Hey," he said after her hello.

"Hey, yourself."

"How you holding up?"

"Like the glue's about to give."

His soft chuckle tickled her ear.

"How about you?"

"Me?" His surprise pleased her.

"Yeah, you."

A pause and then, "I want to see you."

"So meet me."

"Not a good idea."

"Right…"

"Where are you thinking of heading next?"

She scooted out of the way of Tiffany, who came in to access her locker. "I have a class this afternoon. I can skip it…"

"No, go. Just let Dominic know."

"Okay."

Silence. Both because they had nothing more to say…
and everything to say.

"Will I see you later?" she whispered.

"Depends."

"On whether or not you catch Billy."

"On whether or not I catch Billy."

She nodded, but didn't say anything.

They said their goodbyes and then hung up.

For long minutes she sat holding her cell phone in
both hands in her lap. She didn't realize she was in
fellow waitress Tiffany's way until she heard the girl's
dramatic sigh. The area was cramped enough as it
was—with two of them in there it was even more so.

"Are you going to be leaving anytime soon?" Tiffany
asked.

Regina blinked at her. "I was thinking about it."

The girl gave a huge eye roll and then walked from
the room, none too happy with her.

Regina smiled.

DAMN.

Linc watched through the windshield of the van disguised as a general-service cleaning vehicle as Regina
exited the diner, looking a bit timid as she crossed the
street to her Ford. About two cars back sat Dominic. He
thought for a moment that she might wave at the agent,
but thankfully, she caught herself and climbed into her
safe vehicle. He couldn't tell if she was packing the .357
he'd given her last night. He only hoped she was.

"Follow her?" Jason asked from the driver's seat.

"Huh? Oh. No."

"Where to next, then?"

"The Quality Motel."

Jason grimaced as he started the van.

Linc couldn't blame him. They'd hit a dozen like motels in the area in the past two hours with no luck, along with three gas-station convenience stores that had been hit by solo masked robbers. None of the possible leads had panned out. Which is why they'd gone to sit outside the diner at the end of Regina's shift. By sitting back far enough, Linc was hoping to spot Johnson tailing her, as well. It was a remote possibility, since he wasn't likely to follow the same plan twice. But Linc had allowed for the chance that Johnson might think he wouldn't be at the diner again and do just that.

Damn, damn, damn, damn.

Just seeing Regina and not being able to talk to her, see her up close, made him feel as if he had a stomach full of buckshot.

He ran his hands over his face, recognizing the slight signs of fatigue. But there were other symptoms with which he was unfamiliar. Ones directly related to Regina and how he felt about her.

Emotion.

He caught Savage looking at him and he glared back.

"What?"

Jason shrugged, taking a right, away from Regina and where she would be heading to class a couple blocks up. "Nothing. Did I say anything?"

"You didn't have to."

"No, I guess I didn't."

Linc stared through the window at the street and the surrounding cars and pedestrians. "You'd let me know if I'm going off the deep end, wouldn't you?"

"You think I wouldn't?"

"I think you might be scared of an ass whipping, yeah."

Savage threw his head back and howled. "Trust me, if it ever came to that, if the two of us were put in a room together, it's not my ass that would get whipped."

Linc cracked a smile.

"I'm just saying."

"You're just dreaming is more like it."

Savage grinned. "Good thing we get along so well and will never have to find out, huh?"

"Good for you."

He fell silent again.

He felt Jason's hand on his shoulder. "Hey, man, don't worry about it. I'd be the first to tell you. Yeah, while I think emotion is clouding the issues, you're doing exactly what any of us would do in the same situation." He smiled. "Hell, I'm actually glad to see you're human after all."

That was the problem. Right then he was feeling a little too human.

And he didn't like it at all...

22

SHE FELT LIKE a worm pierced three times and squirming on a rusty hook.

Dusk had fallen and Regina paced the length of her narrow apartment and back again, never realizing how small her place was until just that moment.

Of course, she'd never felt imprisoned before, either.

Nothing seemed capable of keeping her attention. Not the television. Not her study materials. Not the radio. All she could think about was that somewhere out there, Billy lurked, waiting to make his next move.

Her every cell shuddered.

She stepped to the curtain and peered through the crack she made. The police had pulled the squad car off night watch. She had the feeling Linc might have had something to do with that, but hadn't asked him during his last call. Their conversations appeared to be getting briefer and briefer, with neither of them quite knowing what to say. It didn't help that her nerves were stretched to the breaking point.

She resumed her pacing.

Her cell phone chirped from the sofa where she'd left it, causing her to jump. She gave an eye roll and picked it up, answering without looking at the display before it bounced to voice mail. She half hoped it was—and wasn't—Linc.

"Hello?"

"Miss Dodson?" a professional-sounding female voice asked.

"Yes."

The caller introduced herself as an emergency-care nurse from the Maine hospital where her mother was checked in. Regina's heart skipped a beat, fearing the worst. She drifted over to the sofa, where she leaned against the arm, her hand slick against the phone.

It took her a moment to realize the nurse had stopped talking.

"Miss Dodson? Are you still there?"

She ran the woman's words over in her mind. She hadn't been told her mother had taken a turn for the worst; she'd been informed she was awake and doing well.

"Yes…yes." Yes!

She knew a relief so complete her legs nearly refused to support her. She paced again, but this time for an entirely different reason.

"Can I speak with her?"

"I suppose a minute wouldn't hurt. But bear in mind she's still groggy…"

LINC FELT LIKE THE worst kind of intruder as he listened to the exchange between Regina and her mother on his cell phone. The conversation wasn't long. And not much was said. But Regina's relief and happiness were so apparent in her tearful words, it made his heart ache. As did the resolve so complete in her promise to come see her as soon as she could.

"I'm thinking about coming home, Mama. For good."

Joan Dodson's voice was weak. "I'd like that, honey. I'd like that a lot…"

Linc closed his phone where he leaned against the van, his throat suddenly tight with emotion.

Regina was considering moving back to Maine?

Jason came out of the motel office, shaking his head. "No go."

Linc pulled in a deep breath and forced the unwanted thoughts away, determined to focus on the situation at hand.

Damn it, Johnson had to be somewhere. He wasn't a ghost capable of appearing on command.

"Where to next?"

Linc rubbed his face with his hands, not having much luck ousting Regina or her words from his mind. "To the compound," he said, fresh out of options.

"Yeah, good idea. Maybe you can grab a couple hours' shut-eye on the cots in the back."

Sleep was the last thing on his list. But he realized it probably wouldn't be a bad idea.

He was surprised when his cell phone rang as he walked around to the passenger's side of the van.

Regina.

He paused before getting into the truck and took her call.

"She's okay."

Her two words the instant he answered made him smile, although the stinging in his chest intensified. "I assume you're talking about your mother."

"Of course, silly. Who else would I be talking about?"

She went over everything he'd essentially just heard, adding her thoughts along the way…and leaving out the part where she'd told her mother she might be coming home.

"I'm sorry. I'm babbling, aren't I?" she said after a long pause.

"Feel free."

"It's just that when I hung up with her, the first person I thought about sharing the good news with was you."

He liked that. He liked that a lot.

"Well…I guess you're busy," she said quietly. "So I won't keep you."

He was busy, but he didn't want her to stop talking. Still, he said, "Okay."

"All right, then. Goodbye."

"Regina?" he said quickly.

"Yes?" He didn't miss the hopeful note in her voice.

"I'm glad she's okay."

He could virtually see her smile. "Thanks. I am, too."

He closed the phone and stood for a long moment, staring at the cars zipping by on the busy avenue, thinking about the randomness of life.

Jason honked the horn.

Linc glared at him through the window before opening the door and climbing into the van.

"Sorry," his partner said.

"My ass. Do it again, and it will be your ass."

Jason's full-throated laugh filled the interior of the vehicle as he put it into gear and pulled out into traffic.

THE FOLLOWING MORNING, Regina was fully prepared to jump out of her skin. While she warmed herself with the knowledge that her mom was doing better, she longed to pack a case and fly to see her, to verify with her own two eyes that she was going to be okay.

Instead, she was locked in her apartment like a bug in a roach motel, her feet stuck to the sticky paper.

Go to work? An option although she wasn't scheduled this early. She normally worked the lunch shift, but that was still a good three hours away.

She picked up her cell phone, began to press the button for Linc, then changed her mind and put the phone down…only to pick it back up a moment later.

It rang before she could dial.

"Linc," she said on an exhale. "I'm going insane."

"I know, baby. I know."

His words and endearment warmed her all over.

She realized the source of her agitation wasn't merely being caged—it was from not being able to see him.

The thought caught her up short. She still hadn't decided whether or not she could forgive him his betrayal. And if she did follow through on her talk of moving back to Maine…

But she had learned a long time ago that oftentimes,

there was a huge disconnect between what the head wanted…and what her heart yearned for.

And her heart wanted Linc.

"We've put together a plan I want to run by you…"

She listened intently as he outlined an idea designed to bring Billy out into the open so Linc could grab him. It should have made her happy that action of some sort was being taken. Instead, she experienced a mix of sadness and fear.

Sadness that Linc thought she had the money.

Fear that Billy thought she did, too.

"Regina?" Linc's voice said softly.

She realized she had yet to respond.

"Is that okay?"

She cleared her throat, blinking back sudden tears as her head and heart did battle yet again. "Um, yes. If you think it's for the best."

"Putting Johnson back behind bars is in everyone's best interest."

She nodded and then said, "Yes."

"Can you be ready in an hour?"

She was ready to have all of this over with now.

She told him yes and then stood for a few minutes after hanging up, a curious numbness stealing over her limbs and robbing her of breath.

The question remained whether or not she was ready for what came after…

LINC DID FORCE HIMSELF to grab a couple of hours of sleep back at the compound, but then was straight at it again, so that when Jason came in at six-thirty, he was ready to hash out the details of the plan he was working on.

It hadn't been an easy decision, putting Regina out there. But he figured she was anyway, whether he liked it or not. While his men were good, there were gaps in coverage that Johnson could take advantage of with a little care and close circumspection. Rather than wait around for Regina's ex to find one, Linc decided it better to set a trap.

It just didn't sit well with him that Regina was the bait.

He sat in the back of the cleaning van monitoring cameras while Jason handled communications. Regina had gone about her day apparently as scheduled—at least to anyone watching—going into work as usual. An hour in, he'd pulled the two vehicles tailing her… and then she'd left the diner after the lunch rush.

He'd questioned whether he should suggest she look antsy, but the moment she emerged from the diner, she appeared more on edge than he was comfortable with.

His back teeth felt fused together as Jason directed the secondary vehicles already in place to follow her.

It seemed to take an agonizing amount of time for Regina to drive the five blocks to the main branch of her bank when in reality it was only a few minutes. He didn't like they'd done it in the middle of the day when traffic was heaviest, but if this was going to work, it had to look as casual as possible. And that meant he couldn't stack the deck too heavily in his favor without tipping Johnson off.

Just before Regina was to turn the final corner, Jason

directed Megan to come out of a nearby restaurant and get into her car, freeing up a spot directly across the street from the bank. Thankfully the financial institution was situated in the middle of a solid block of side-by-side buildings, which meant no hidden access. If Johnson nabbed her, he'd have to do so in plain sight. And that was exactly when Linc planned to grab the son of a bitch and send him back to prison where he belonged.

The plan was that Regina would go in and access a safe-deposit box set up in her name earlier in the day. A bag of money had been placed there and she was to take it out and then leave the bank, the bag in clear sight of anyone watching.

He absently rubbed the back of his neck, remembering how she'd visibly blanched when he outlined that part of the plan.

Regina parked her car as planned. But she didn't immediately get out.

"What's she doing?" Jason asked after a few minutes.

Linc squinted at the cameras poised at different angles. "I don't know."

"You don't think Johnson gained access to her car again?"

He shook his head. "No. I got a camera in there, too. See."

The shot showed she was by herself. She seemed to be toying with her cell phone and then answered it. Linc fumbled to take his out of his pocket, flicking it open. The number was blocked; the ID read Private. He punched the button to listen in on her conversation.

"…I want you to do exactly as I say…"

Johnson.

Shit!

Linc shouted for someone to get on a trace, double time…

23

REGINA SWORE SHE could feel Billy's breath on her ear even though they were speaking on the phone. She wiped her slick palms on the front of her waitress uniform, listening as he spoke. She began to look in the rearview mirror, trying to make out where Linc might be then reminded herself not to. She wasn't supposed to appear as if she was aware anyone else was around.

"What do you want?" she whispered.

His taunting laugh touched her with icy fingers. "I want you to go into that bank and get my money. I'll call you with the rest when you get out."

"The police are watching me," she lied.

"No, they're not. They pulled patrol yesterday morning. But your boyfriend is watching. Now go in and do your business."

As soon as she hung up, the phone vibrated. She pressed the button for speaker as Linc had directed her to.

"He's bluffing. He doesn't know I'm behind you."

"What if you're wrong?"

"I'm not."

"What do I do now?"

"Exactly as we talked about."

It didn't hit her until that moment what exactly she was doing. She was tempting the devil himself out of the shadows.

"He's taking the bait, Regina. This will be over soon."

That's what she was afraid of...

LINC HAD LITTLE DOUBT Johnson was somewhere nearby. The knowledge edged up his adrenaline level. This was going to work.

"Get a lock on that cell?" he asked.

Jason shook his head. "No. Couldn't home in on it before he cut off."

Johnson had probably popped the battery the instant he disconnected, making any signal trace impossible. In fact, he wouldn't be surprised if the man was using more than one cell phone for whatever he had in mind.

Linc paced the narrow length of the van and then leaned over to stare at the monitors, watching the front of the bank. Regina had looked and sounded more spooked than he had expected. Not that he could blame her, considering her last encounter with her no-good ex. Still, he battled an incredible urge to pull her out now and go back to trying to track Johnson in a way that had nothing to do with her.

"Here she comes," Jason said unnecessarily, because Linc was already watching her exit the bank's front doors clutching the bag they'd planted.

She watched for traffic and then crossed to her car.

"Okay, he's going to be calling again. Be at the ready," Linc told the crew.

Only, Billy didn't call.

Regina sat in the car for a good five minutes in silence.

Linc called her and she answered immediately.

"What now?" she asked.

He didn't want her going back to the diner. He didn't want her anywhere out in public, period. Not because of the money—although that was a factor—but because he wanted her to be somewhere he could better protect her.

"Go home."

"My place?"

"Yes."

She disconnected and Jason shared the change in destination to the tails.

Damn. What was Johnson doing?

"That's a hundred grand of Lazarus money she's carrying," Jason said casually.

Linc stared at him.

"Just sayin'."

"Yeah, well, don't."

Savage shrugged and went back to directing the agents tailing her. One in front, two more behind and then, of course, them in the van.

He hated being so far behind her, but he didn't dare risk getting closer for fear Johnson would spot him.

But odds were pretty good he already had.

The bank robbery Billy "the Bank Robber" Johnson had pulled in Boston had been a simple, straightforward deal, with little technology involved. But a check of what he'd been up to in prison verified Johnson had been busy bringing himself up to speed on modern tech. Book requests, electronics classes and computer logs had shown he'd taken quite an interest in his new pastime.

Linc would never have imagined he'd come so far so fast.

Ten minutes later, Regina parked at the curb outside her house and one tail drove past her to change places with the lead while the other pulled into a driveway a block and a half back.

"Chief?" Jason asked.

Linc ran his hand over his close-cropped hair, watching as cameras were readjusted, giving him a clean shot of Regina getting out of her car and walking to her apartment.

"Pass and park up a block."

"He'll spot us."

"You think?" He pulled in a calming breath. "I'm betting he already knows we're here. Better to be out in plain sight."

"Got ya."

Jason directed the driver to do as he asked and Linc opened the partition to the cab and leaned between the seats, staring through the windshield. As they passed, Regina looked over her shoulder, staring directly at him. The fear in her eyes was apparent. It was all he could do not to order the vehicle to stop so he could get out and go inside with her.

He went back to the control panel. "Anyone got anything?" he demanded.

Answers came back in the negative. No one had spotted anything out of the ordinary.

It appeared Johnson was a ghost…

REGINA FELT INSTANTLY better once she was inside her own apartment with the alarm system armed.

She stood in the middle of the living room, still clutching the bag of money to her stomach. She stared at it and then put it down on the coffee table, her hands suddenly feeling dirty. She went into the bathroom and ran hot water, pumping a double helping of soap into her palm and scrubbing thoroughly. She looked at herself in the mirror and gave a start. She looked tired and scared. Both of which she was, of course. She merely hadn't expected to see evidence of it on her face.

She dried her hands and took the pins out of her hair, fluffing the curly strands until she looked somewhat better.

Her cell vibrated. She lifted it to her ear thinking she didn't have to put it on speaker again.

"What now?" she asked.

"Sit tight. Wait for him to contact you again."

"No luck spotting him?"

A pause and then a solemn, "No."

She pressed Disconnect and then leaned against the sink, giving in to the urge to close her eyes, however briefly.

Last night had been a long one. But now that a plan was actually in motion and Billy had contacted her, she felt better. She grimaced. "Better" didn't quite make the grade. Rather, she felt…hopeful that all this would soon be over.

Still, she couldn't help being afraid of what might happen next.

She opened the medicine cabinet and shook out a couple of pain relievers into her hand, then filled a cup with water. She closed the mirror—and started when she found she wasn't alone in the room…

LINC COULDN'T REMEMBER a time when he'd felt more ill at ease…more out of control over a situation.

"Hang loose, man. We've got this covered," Jason said from his seat at the communications panel.

"Something's not right."

"Of course it's not. There's some nutcase who's got an X marked on your girl."

Linc stared at the monitors. "No…no. It's something else."

"There is nothing else. She went into the apartment. She's safe."

Linc's stomach dropped. Suddenly, he knew. He checked his firearm and made for the back doors.

"Where in the hell you going?"

"The son of a bitch is in there…"

REGINA'S HEART POUNDED so hard against her rib cage she was half-afraid it would break right through.

Billy leered at her. "Yeah, figured you and your boyfriend were expecting me to make a move on the street. No one expected me to be here." He held the gun he'd had the other day in one hand and the money bag in the other. "I was afraid this would be a ruse, but it's not, is it?" He shook it. "Only I'm guessing it's not all here. Where's the rest of it?"

"There is no more," Regina said, wishing she had thought to bring her own firearm in with her. She'd taken it off and left it in the car when she went into the bank. It still sat in her locked glove box, well out of reach and useless to her.

Billy stepped closer to her, his breath even more rancid than it had been the other day. Either that or she was more aware of it since he was standing in front of her rather than behind.

He maneuvered the bag so he was holding it with his right hand along with the gun and grabbed her chin, squeezing tight. "Where's the rest of it?"

She jerked herself free of his grip. "That's it. That's all of it."

She searched her brain for every self-defense move she'd learned over the past year and a half, but there was very little maneuvering room. He'd caught her off guard, rendering her capable of only reaction, not action.

"Move," he said, motioning toward the bathroom door.

She eyed her cell phone on the sink counter.

"Leave it."

She did. "You'll never get out of here. You know that, don't you?" she taunted, which probably wasn't a good idea, but she couldn't help herself.

"Sounds awfully close to 'my boyfriend's going to beat you up,' for comfort, babe." He grabbed her arm from behind and for a brief moment she was flush against him. The meager contents of her stomach rushed up into her throat at his obvious arousal. "But right now, I'm your boyfriend." He pressed his face against her neck. "Miss me? I missed you. Can't wait to show you how much…"

Her cell rang in the other room. Billy drew back to look at it, giving her just the opportunity she needed. She grabbed his right hand and pushed it down, stomping on his foot at the same time. He made a low growl but otherwise was unfazed outside a slight stumble back.

But that slight stumble was all she needed to put some much-needed distance between them, no matter how much the gun negated it. At least he was no longer touching her.

Just then the front door swung open wide and Linc filled the space.

"Down on all fours like the dog you are, Johnson. Your ass is mine…"

24

LINC HATED BEING RIGHT. Seeing Johnson standing so near Regina, much less in the same room, made his gut wrench and his trigger finger itchier than he'd ever felt it. Blood rushed past his ears, making it nearly impossible to hear anything outside of it.

"I said get down! Now!" he repeated.

But Johnson wasn't having any of it. He merely leered at him, his own gun solidly pointed at Regina where she stood near her bedroom door, her beautiful face a portrait in fear.

Linc took a step closer, then another. He was going to get this bastard, one way or another.

He made eye contact with Regina, holding her gaze until she finally seemed to see him. Then he nodded slightly toward her bedroom.

The instant she dived out of the line of fire, Linc jumped on Johnson, bringing his shooting arm down and aiming to knock his legs out from under him. But Johnson was ready, his legs squared, and while his gun was pointed toward the floor, he demonstrated the type of fight that had gotten him this far. Not only was he holding his own, he managed to turn toward Linc.

The side of Johnson's gun connected with Linc's jaw, a solid pistol whip that inspired stars that disappeared as quickly as they appeared. Focusing on keeping the firearm in question in no position to shoot Regina or him, he wrestled the convict upright.

"Ain't no way you're taking me again, Willams. Not a chance in hell."

"Says who?" Linc worked on getting him to drop the gun.

"Says me. I'd rather die than go back to that rat hole."

"Yes, well, the choice is yours."

Finally, Johnson's gun clanked to the floor as the result of Linc's efforts and he quickly kicked it away so that it skidded short of the bedroom door. He couldn't make out Regina; he guessed she was huddling around the corner out of range. Which left him free to do what he needed.

He brought his boot down hard against Johnson's knee. The man groaned in pain. Linc moved his leg around and hit the back of the same joint, satisfied when he heard a sharp crack. Johnson dropped to all fours. Linc slammed his boot between the man's shoulder blades, shoving him to lie flat on the floor.

"Your first mistake?" he said. "Breaking out of prison. Second? Coming after Regina."

He positioned himself so he could lean back to look into the bedroom, finding Regina flat against the wall just inside.

Johnson struggled against his hold.

Linc brought his gun down until the barrel was lined up with the back of his head.

"What?" Johnson spat a mouthful of blood onto the rug. "You're not going to shoot me."

"What makes you so sure?"

"Because you can't shoot without cause. You're a goddamn government cop!"

"Not anymore I'm not. You should have been a little more thorough with your research, Johnson."

"That Lazarus shit don't meaning nothing. Once a cop, always a freakin' cop, no matter if it's federal. Your ass will be in a heap of trouble if you squeeze off a round."

Linc's finger itched so badly he rubbed it against the trigger.

Johnson was right in one aspect. As an FBI agent, he'd been trained to hold himself in check, to stop just short of what was essentially execution. However, Billy was overlooking the fact that assassination had essentially been his job in the service.

And it was that instinct, that desire to rid the world of an unredeemable son of a bitch who would not only not be missed, but whose death might be celebrated, that made his pulse beat even stronger.

If keeping the piece of shit away from Regina entered anywhere into the equation, he wasn't going to address it just then.

"Linc…"

Jason said his name from the front doorway. Two other recruits were already inside the apartment, their guns drawn. Johnson wasn't going anywhere.

"He's not worth it, man. You know they'll put him

under extra security after this. He'll never be free again."

The part of Linc's mind still working recognized the rational thought. The animal part wanted nothing more than to pull the trigger.

Damn.

He withdrew the gun and took a deep breath. Then another. Slowly, the world began to tilt right again.

He stepped over his prey...and Johnson wildly grabbed for his gun in a last-ditch effort for freedom.

A round went off and grazed one of the two guys in the room.

Another gunshot rang out. But this time, it hadn't come from his gun. Linc looked behind him to see Regina had picked up Johnson's firearm, holding it straight out in front of her, the barrel aimed toward her ex.

Linc was aware of Johnson going limp. His hand slipped away and dropped to the floor.

Linc recognized the lethal shot to the back of the head and dropped his guard.

Jason had been right: Billy "the Bank Robber" Johnson wouldn't be free again...

HOURS LATER, REGINA still shook, albeit more inside than out.

Linc had taken her to a downtown hotel after she'd refused to go back to his place. She now sat on the edge of the king-size bed wrapped in a white robe, her hair in a towel, even though she'd taken a shower nearly an hour ago.

Nearby, Linc was on the phone, presumably doing a follow-up report on what had gone down at her apartment, although she barely registered what was being said.

She closed her eyes and rubbed the heel of her hands against them, trying to scrub away the image of Billy lying lifeless on her living room floor.

Trying to erase the fact she was the responsible for his being that way.

She'd killed Billy...

She tried to work out what happened. One minute he'd been on the floor, immobilized; the next he was fighting Linc for his gun and a man was shot...

She'd acted on pure instinct when she'd picked up Billy's gun and pulled the trigger. She'd only meant to disable him.

Instead, she'd killed him.

"Regina?"

It wasn't until she heard Linc say her name that she realized he'd finished his phone conversation. There were no other sounds in the room outside the hum of the air conditioner. The television was off. The radio silent.

She felt him sit down next to her.

"You're cold," he remarked.

She was. But it wasn't the type of cold a blanket or hot shower could banish.

He reached for where her hands were in her lap and rubbed them in his. She immediately felt better... warmer.

Still, something compelled her to tug her fingers out of his grip.

"The first time is always hard," he said quietly.

She squinted at him. Who said words like that?

The realization that she knew very little about him rang like a bell in the back of her head. That flip side of her experiencing the sensation of being safe in his arms came with a price, as well as a story.

"Sounds like you're suggesting there's going to be a second," she whispered.

He grimaced and ran his hands over his head. "Not unless Johnson finds a way to break out of hell."

She winced.

"Damn. I'm sorry. That was wrong of me to say."

She shook her head. "That's okay."

Billy Johnson may have been hell-worthy, but she'd loved him once. Or at least, she'd thought she had. He'd been her first date. Her first kiss. Her first time. She'd believed he deserved punishment for his many crimes. But she never would have imagined it would have been death at her own hands.

"I guess my shooting at the range wasn't a fluke," she whispered, hot tears scorching her cheeks.

Linc placed his hand against her back.

"I only wanted to stop him…" She swallowed hard. "No, that's not right. I wasn't thinking anything. I only reacted."

"That's right. Remember that—you didn't do it on purpose."

She stared at him. "But that doesn't change what happened."

He didn't say anything for a long time, then he shook his head. "No, it doesn't."

The numbness surrounding her dissolved and she felt as if her insides collapsed. Linc folded her into his big arms and she let him, glad for the support while gusts of grief blew through her.

She'd taken care of Billy for so long, she'd had to physically remove herself from his immediate vicinity to put a halt to it. How did one go from being a nurturer to being a killer, seemingly within the blink of an eye?

Justifiable homicide. Self-defense. It didn't matter what everyone else labeled her actions; she knew what she was.

"You don't blame yourself for his crimes?" Linc asked after she'd calmed down enough to hear him over her sobs, but not enough to move away from him. If anything, she burrowed farther into his chest, clutching the soft cotton of his black T-shirt in her fist.

She shook her head. "No. I may have years ago. I'd thought there was something I was doing wrong, some way I could make life better for him, prevent him from making the choices he did. But that was a long time ago…"

Then it occurred to her: What would happen to Billy now?

She drew back and wiped her cheeks first with her hands and then with the sleeve of her robe.

"What's going to happen to his body?"

Linc blinked. "I don't know. I suppose since he was still officially a prisoner of the state, they'll see to his remains."

"His family?"

"I thought you said he didn't have anyone outside of his father?"

She looked down into her lap. "He doesn't."

"I guess his family could petition for…custody…" He offered up an apologetic smile. "Sorry, that's not my area of expertise."

"And what is, exactly?"

He didn't respond.

"I mean, I know you were a Marine. And an FBI agent. But…" She shivered. "I saw something today that scared me. For a moment, it was like I didn't know you." She worried her bottom lip between her teeth. "Then again, I don't, do I? Not really."

"You know what matters."

"Do I?" She shook her head. "Because right now I don't think I do."

She began to get up.

"Where are you going?"

"I…I need to see what's going to happen to Billy's body. I think it appropriate he be buried at home."

"You're not thinking about handling it?"

She frowned at him. "Why not?"

"Haven't you done enough for him?"

"What? By killing him?"

"By protecting yourself. And everyone else in the room."

"By killing him."

Silence fell between them.

"I don't expect you to understand, Linc."

"I understand you're feeling guilty."

"No." She stared at the open windows and the building across the street. "Yes. I suppose guilt is there somewhere. But that's not what's motivating me now." She smiled at him, but he was little more than a blur through her tears. "It's the last thing I'll ever have to do for him. And I need to do it."

He nodded, but his expression told her he didn't understand at all.

It didn't matter. She felt compelled to do it. She feared if she didn't, she'd never find peace.

If there was any peace to be found.

"Regina?"

She turned back toward him, stopping just outside the bathroom where she'd been going to get dressed.

"You said you don't know me. You're right. I'm not..." He got up and paced in the opposite direction. "Voluntarily offering up information about myself is not something I've ever really done."

She waited.

"But I think it's important you know this..."

25

THAT WAS IT. The reason why he hadn't wanted to tell Regina he was tailing Johnson. The way she looked at him now, as if he were a stranger, twisted like razor wire in his gut.

What he was about to tell her, he had told no one. Not even his aunt. But he needed to tell Regina now. Not toward any end; he feared it was already too late for that. But because he needed to share it with her.

He walked back to the bed and sat down on the foot, resting his head in his hands for a few moments before looking back up at her.

"My father was the guard Johnson shot during the bank robbery."

There, he'd said it.

He hadn't expected it to be easy. But he hadn't expected to feel as if a hole had just been blown in his chest, either.

"I don't understand…"

Regina's words were soft, soothing the open wound.

"Trust me, at the time I didn't, either." He dropped his head back and closed his eyes, remembering the case.

Reviewing security CDs. Witness reports. Trying to get a line on the bank robber's identity. It had been just another run-of-the-mill case to him as an FBI agent—until the security man's name jumped out at him. Looking closer, the man's gestures and mannerisms looked far too familiar. "I didn't know when it happened. He was just another victim when I started working the case. Hell, I never even knew my father. Never felt compelled to look for him. As far as I knew, he was still bouncing around New York somewhere. The last place I expected to encounter him was in Boston."

In a morgue.

He didn't say the words aloud. The stark memory of standing over Lincoln Williams Sr.'s motionless body that day was forever etched in his mind. The empty space inside him was filled with the ghostly image and unacknowledged emotions.

He hadn't been aware Regina had joined him on the bed until he felt her hand on his arm.

"I'm sorry…"

He took a deep breath. "Yeah. Thanks."

The words sounded casual, but they were anything but.

"I should have resigned the case on the spot, you know, at the moment of discovery. But…"

"But you couldn't. You wanted to find your father's killer."

He nodded, although "wanted" fell far short of the mark. He *needed* to find his father's killer. And as earlier in the day, had he been alone, he would have killed Billy Johnson with little remorse.

"I'm sorry."

He nodded, staring at his hands between his knees.

She squeezed his arm.

"I'm sorry Billy robbed you of any chance you might have had of meeting your father when he was still alive."

He looked at her and suddenly that gaping hole pulsed and began to fill with everything that was her.

He wanted to kiss her. To give the wild and tangled emotions within him a physical release. To demonstrate his gratitude for her warmth and understanding.

To show her he loved her.

He dipped his head down, paused, hesitant. He didn't know if she'd welcome his kiss.

She tilted her chin upward, meeting his lips softly.

Linc groaned deep in his stomach and caressed her cheek, deepening the kiss.

He was coming to need this woman in a way that frightened him more than facing any ten enemies.

He slid his hand down her neck and then inside the front of her robe, seeking and finding her breasts.

Her soft gasp wrapped itself around him.

He began pushing the robe from her shoulders...

And she gently grasped his arms and pulled back from their kiss.

The sober shadow in her eyes hit him like a fist to the stomach.

"I...I can't," she whispered.

As she got up and hurried toward the bathroom, he knew a fear that he might never be with her again...

WHEN REGINA EMERGED from the bathroom a half hour later, dressed and looking somewhat more human—if not quite anywhere near feeling that way—she was alone. She looked for a note, but didn't find one.

For a long time, she stood in front of the windows staring out at nothing, thinking about the man who had managed to become such an integral part of her life over the past couple weeks.

She had never thought of herself as lonely until she met him. Now...

She hugged herself tightly.

Now, she needed to focus on what needed to be done.

26

"WHERE DO YOU want these?"

Five days later, Regina stood staring out the back kitchen window of her mother's small, two-bedroom bungalow; the house she'd grown up in. The scene was familiar, but…different somehow.

Or perhaps it wasn't the view that was different, but rather her.

She seemed to be doing a lot of gazing through windows lately. Looking at life from the inside out. Reviewing it. Considering it through eyes affected by recent events.

She glanced over her shoulder to where Vivienne was holding the two bags of groceries she'd brought in from the rental car. She went to help.

"Here." She accepted one of the bags, then put it on the yellow linoleum table, disturbing the doily her mother had stretched across it. She was mildly surprised to find herself staring at the initials she had carved into the surface nearly ten years ago: RD + BJ = TLF (Regina Dodson + Billy Johnson = True Love Forever).

Her heart hiccuped. Not for love lost, but rather for lost innocence.

She absently ran her fingertip over the deep grooves she'd made with her house key. At some point after their breakup, she'd considered turning BJ into a BB and making a butterfly out of the letters. Then she realized there wouldn't be much point in that; she'd always know what was really there.

"Hey," Viv said, putting her hand on her shoulder. "You going to be okay?"

Regina took a deep breath, covered the initial again and then smiled at her friend. "Yeah. I'm beginning to think I will."

After Linc left the hotel that day, she hadn't heard from him again. And when she'd needed someone, she'd forced herself to reach out to Vivienne instead. Her friend had risen to the occasion, insisting she travel back to Maine with her to help.

As for Linc…

Her gaze drifted back to the initials on the table, the fear that had gripped her in the hotel room returning; not as strongly, but still there.

While she would never compare Linc to Billy…she was able to compare herself to the woman she used to be. She was coming to recognize that when she gave herself, she gave herself fully, without thought to consequences or caution. It didn't take a Ph.D to know that hadn't exactly worked out well with her first relationship, did it?

"The florist called to verify the order for tomorrow," Viv said. "Good thing she did, because she accidentally flipped the number of flowers in the arrangement. It would have doubled the price. I straightened her out."

Flowers…

While she suspected a few townsfolk and perhaps high school friends would come out for the funeral scheduled for tomorrow, she doubted any of them would send flowers. And the majority would likely attend more out of curiosity than anything else. So she'd ordered them herself.

As for Billy's father… Well, when she'd called from Colorado to tell him the news, and asked if he wanted to be involved in the arrangements, he'd muttered something unpleasant and hung up on her. Which she'd taken to mean no. Still, she'd gone to visit him yesterday to give him the funeral details in case he'd like to attend. He hadn't said a word to her before closing the door, but she could tell by his red-rimmed eyes he was taking the news hard.

Either that, or the bottle he'd always been so fond of had bitten him hard.

Probably a little of both. Or a lot.

The only one who hadn't questioned her sanity when it came to bringing Billy home and seeing to his funeral arrangements had been her mother.

She smiled fondly, thinking of the woman napping in her outdated, pink-painted bedroom. When she'd shared what she had in mind, Joan had merely smiled, hugged her and told her she loved her. Then asked what she could do.

Her mother had been released from the hospital three days ago, a little weak and bearing the scars of her ordeal, some of which would go away, others that probably never would. But she hadn't breathed a word about the pain Billy had caused them both. Regina had been the one to ask her mom where she'd found the strength.

"It's not strength, sweetie, it's acceptance. Besides, there's no sense holding a grudge against someone who's no longer with us…"

Regina began putting the groceries away, not noticing Viv had left the room until she came back in, holding something in her hands.

"Wow. Is this him?"

She'd seen the photo her mother had framed of her and Billy sitting on the dining room cabinet, but hadn't had the heart to take it down.

Regina put eggs and milk away in the refrigerator and then closed the door. "Yeah. Just after I graduated high school."

"Is it bad taste to say he was hot?"

She smiled faintly. "I think you just did, so what does it matter?"

Viv finally looked up from the frame and at her. "I'm sorry. Should I throw it away?"

"No." She stepped to take the picture from her friend, staring at it for a long moment. So young. Life stretched out before them like a glistening, freshly paved road inviting them to ride it. And ride it they did. For a short time.

She took the picture out of the frame and put both on the table. Maybe her mom would put it in one of the old photo albums. She could use the frame for something else.

"So," Regina said, taking a deep breath and smiling. "We can leave the ham for the morning. You ready to help me put together veggie and cheese trays and potato salad for the hordes that'll probably not show up to pay their respects after the service tomorrow?"

"I heard people from the church are planning to come," Viv said.

"Oh?"

Her friend smiled. "Yeah. The nice owner of the service station up the road told me."

"Which means he'll probably be coming...?"

Viv smiled and batted her eyes as she pulled the band from the broccoli. "One can hope."

The ache in Regina's chest pulsed as she tried not to think of someone else she wished would be there...

THE DAY OF THE funeral dawned hot and bright. Regina had thought of every detail, except what she was going to wear. As a general rule, she avoided black, finding nothing basic in a shade that drained her complexion of all color. So she was forced to borrow something from Viv, who, it appeared, had brought five different outfits from which to choose for the day...and explained the two large suitcases she'd brought along for a five-day trip.

Of course, Regina wasn't sure how she felt about the tightness or the sexy cut of the black sundress, but she hadn't had time to buy anything else. She just had to remind herself to stop fussing with it.

So there she stood at the grave site, listening to the pastor's quiet voice as he spoke to the five people present. The church service had been quiet, but moderately attended, most offering their apologies for not going to the burial because of the heat.

Billy's dad hadn't made an appearance at either place.

Viv stood on one side of her, her mother on the other. Across from them stood one of Billy's old high school teachers and an elderly woman her mother said was a church regular who attended every funeral. Her hat was bright yellow and the sun hitting it made her look as if she was wearing an extra-large halo.

Her mother leaned closer to her. "Look off to your right…about five rows back."

Regina did. And was surprised to find Billy's father there, dressed in an old black suit at least a size too small, holding a hat in his hands.

Viv leaned in from the other direction. "I saw him at the service, too. At the back of the church. He left before it was over."

Regina wasn't sure why she was glad he'd come. Perhaps because she hoped it might help him cope with the loss of his only son. Or maybe she felt better knowing that Billy had at least one family member there.

The pastor concluded the reading. Regina stepped forward and laid the red rose she held on the simple casket. She closed her eyes briefly, silently wishing Billy peace.

The other attendees followed suit while she sought out Mr. Johnson's gaze. He was wiping his eyes with the back of his hand, but when he spotted her watching him, he quickly turned and walked in the opposite direction.

She dropped her gaze, wanting to invite him back to the house for something to eat, but respecting his need for privacy.

Viv linked her arm in hers. "Now let's get back to the house and see what yummy tidbits end up on the buffet."

Regina shook her head. "You're impossible."

"Yeah, but you love me anyway."

Regina smiled and leaned her head against Viv's. That, she did.

But as they walked toward the car, she spotted someone else who had secretly attended the burial. Someone she hadn't seen in five days. The one person she had wanted to see the most.

Viv stopped midchatter and followed her gaze. Her mother stopped. "Is something wrong?"

Viv released Regina's arm and took her mother's instead. "No. I'd say something is very, very right. Come, Joan, why don't we get out of these two kids' way."

Regina distantly listened as her mother asked Viv who the handsome young man was, unable to respond because her heart was beating so loudly it impeded her hearing and vocalization abilities.

Somehow her feet carried her to where Linc stood next to a black SUV looking awkward and cautious.

She stopped a foot away, absently folding her arms across her chest. "Um, hi," she said softly.

"Hi, yourself."

She glanced at the SUV, trying to distract herself from how good he looked. "Drive that here?"

He smiled. "Rental."

She cleared her throat. "How long you staying?"

"Don't know yet."

She squinted at him, trying to decide if she wanted

to know more or if she should move on with her day, which wasn't yet finished.

"I guess I don't have to ask if you came for the funeral," she said quietly.

"No, Regina, you don't. We both know I came for you."

She chewed on the inside of her lip and glanced at where her mother and Viv had already gotten into the car. They'd driven her rental car rather than her mother's old Buick, which wasn't equipped to handle unusual, hot days in Maine.

"Walk with me a minute?" he asked.

"I, um…"

"Please?"

Her breath hitched and in that one moment she couldn't have refused him anything.

They began walking through the grass, away from the cars, neither of them saying anything.

Then Regina felt compelled to break the silence… "I'm coming home."

He looked at her.

"You know, moving back here."

His frown was deep. "When?"

She shrugged. "After classes end in August."

He nodded as if the news didn't surprise him.

"Can I ask you something?" She stopped under the shade of an old maple and turned toward him.

He nodded.

"Do you really think I kept that money?"

His gaze never faltered. "No. Not for a minute."

"Not for a second?"

He cracked a small smile. "Maybe a second. What did you do with it?"

"Does it matter?"

"No. No, I guess it doesn't. Because I'm guessing whatever it was, it was a good cause."

His words warmed her heart.

She remembered vividly sitting with all that money before her on her bed, behind her closed door, trying to overcome the shock of seeing so much cash, grappling with the guilt associated with the unseen blood that marred it, and working out what she should do with it.

Ultimately, she'd divided it up into three uneven piles and then put each in separate envelopes. The largest she'd placed in the mailbox of the disabled-for-life security guard who'd survived. The other two she'd given to a church and a charity that specialized in dealing with underprivileged youth.

Linc listened silently as she told him.

"I would have given it to your father's family, had he had one. But from what I could understand, well, he was alone."

He looked away. "Yes. Yes, he was."

She reached out and placed her hand on his arm. They stood silently for a long time.

"Can I ask you something else?" she finally said. "Why did you come all this way?"

He searched her face. "Isn't it obvious?" His words were so quiet, she almost didn't hear them. "I needed to see you."

She forced a swallow down her tight throat. "Why?"

He reached out, tucking a curl that had escaped her band behind her ear, the backs of his knuckles lingering against her skin. "To remind myself that what happened between us wasn't a dream."

Regina's skin heated in a way that had nothing to do with the air temperature.

"To tell you… No, to thank you."

"For what?"

"For seeing me."

IT HADN'T BEEN EASY coming to Maine, taking the risk Regina might not want him around. But it would have been harder still not to come.

They'd stopped walking and Linc watched the way the sunlight played on her soft hair through the leaves of the tree. Her expression was warm but questioning.

"I'm not sure I know what you mean…" She trailed off.

He looked down at his feet, wondering when he'd last worn anything other than boots. "I'm not sure I'm capable of explaining it." He smiled wryly. "I'm not used to this…communication stuff. At least not when it comes to emotions…"

"I think you're doing okay."

"Then why are you considering staying here in Maine?"

This time she looked away.

"Sorry. See? I've already mucked things up."

She shook her head. "No, no, you haven't. Please… continue."

He wanted to kiss her so badly he ached with the need. "I was invisible."

Her brows drew together.

"I don't mean like Invisible Man invisible—that would be rubber-room material." She laughed quietly. "I'm saying that for as long as I can remember, I felt like I could easily blend into the background. As if I wasn't even there."

She squinted. "I'm guessing that skill came in handy in the military...and beyond."

He nodded. "Yes. But when it came to my personal life..."

"It carried over," she said simply.

"Yes."

"I understand. I think all of us have experienced that sensation from time to time."

He searched her face, grateful she was trying to make it easier for him, even though she had every reason not to. "Yes, but in my case it was all the time, a way of life."

He reached out to touch the side of her face, hesitating as if to ask permission. She leaned in the rest of the way. Something inside him sighed wide-open at the contact.

"Until you," he whispered. "From day one...well, you saw me. Sensed when I was present. Sought me out..." He chuckled without humor. "Made tailing you hard as hell..."

She covered his hand with hers.

"Then when we met, there was no escaping you. You were everywhere. Inside me, outside..."

"I felt the same way. As if you understood me like no one else could." She stroked his fingers with hers.

"I think it's natural, that feeling. You know, when two people are falling…"

He raised a brow, waiting…no, hoping, she would say it.

She didn't. So he did: "In love? Falling in love?"

She dropped her gaze and nodded.

"Do you love me, Regina?"

She swallowed hard.

"Because I sure as hell love you."

He didn't know who moved first, but they were suddenly embracing.

He could feel her heart thudding against his, her scent filling his entire being.

"How long are you planning to stay?" she asked quietly.

He tilted her chin up and kissed her lingeringly. "For as long as you'll have me."

He'd already worked all that out in the hope she'd let him stay; let him be a part of her life.

He could work from anywhere, so long as he had a laptop and his cell phone. He'd have to travel frequently, but he planned to do as little of that as possible. From here on out he knew what was important. And he intended to make sure she understood that.

"I love you, Linc," she whispered. "I wouldn't be opposed to the idea of you staying forever."

And just like that, he knew he'd never be invisible again.

* * * * *

COMING NEXT MONTH

Blaze's 10th Anniversary
Special Collectors' Editions

Available July 26, 2011

#627 THE BRADDOCK BOYS: TRAVIS
Love at First Bite
Kimberly Raye

#628 HOTSHOT
Uniformly Hot!
Jo Leigh

#629 UNDENIABLE PLEASURES
The Pleasure Seekers
Tori Carrington

#630 COWBOYS LIKE US
Sons of Chance
Vicki Lewis Thompson

#631 TOO HOT TO TOUCH
Legendary Lovers
Julie Leto

#632 EXTRA INNINGS
Encounters
Debbi Rawlins

You can find more information on upcoming
Harlequin® titles, free excerpts and more at
www.HarlequinInsideRomance.com.

REQUEST YOUR FREE BOOKS!
2 FREE NOVELS PLUS 2 FREE GIFTS!

red-hot reads!

YES! Please send me 2 FREE Harlequin® Blaze™ novels and my 2 FREE gifts (gifts are worth about $10). After receiving them, if I don't wish to receive any more books, I can return the shipping statement marked "cancel." If I don't cancel, I will receive 6 brand-new novels every month and be billed just $4.49 per book in the U.S. or $4.96 per book in Canada. That's a saving of at least 14% off the cover price. It's quite a bargain. Shipping and handling is just 50¢ per book in the U.S. and 75¢ per book in Canada.* I understand that accepting the 2 free books and gifts places me under no obligation to buy anything. I can always return a shipment and cancel at any time. Even if I never buy another book, the two free books and gifts are mine to keep forever.

151/351 HDN FEQE

Name	(PLEASE PRINT)	
Address		Apt. #
City	State/Prov.	Zip/Postal Code

Signature (if under 18, a parent or guardian must sign)

Mail to the **Reader Service:**
IN U.S.A.: P.O. Box 1867, Buffalo, NY 14240-1867
IN CANADA: P.O. Box 609, Fort Erie, Ontario L2A 5X3

Not valid for current subscribers to Harlequin Blaze books.

Want to try two free books from another line?
Call 1-800-873-8635 or visit www.ReaderService.com.

* Terms and prices subject to change without notice. Prices do not include applicable taxes. Sales tax applicable in N.Y. Canadian residents will be charged applicable taxes. Offer not valid in Quebec. This offer is limited to one order per household. All orders subject to credit approval. Credit or debit balances in a customer's account(s) may be offset by any other outstanding balance owed by or to the customer. Please allow 4 to 6 weeks for delivery. Offer available while quantities last.

Your Privacy—The Reader Service is committed to protecting your privacy. Our Privacy Policy is available online at www.ReaderService.com or upon request from the Reader Service.

We make a portion of our mailing list available to reputable third parties that offer products we believe may interest you. If you prefer that we not exchange your name with third parties, or if you wish to clarify or modify your communication preferences, please visit us at www.ReaderService.com/consumerschoice or write to us at Reader Service Preference Service, P.O. Box 9062, Buffalo, NY 14269. Include your complete name and address.

HBI1B

*Once bitten, twice shy. That's Gabby Wade's motto—
especially when it comes to Adamson men.
And the moment she meets Jon Adamson her theory
is confirmed. But with each encounter a little* something
*sparks between them, making her wonder if she's been
too hasty to dismiss this one!*

*Enjoy this sneak peek from ONE GOOD REASON
by Sarah Mayberry, available August 2011
from Harlequin® Superromance®.*

Gabby Wade's heartbeat thumped in her ears as she marched to her office. She wanted to pretend it was because of her brisk pace returning from the file room, but she wasn't that good a liar.

Her heart was beating like a tom-tom because Jon Adamson had touched her. In a very male, very possessive way. She could still feel the heat of his big hand burning through the seat of her khakis as he'd steadied her on the ladder.

It had taken every ounce of self-control to tell him to unhand her. What she'd really wanted was to grab him by his shirt and, well, explore all those urges his touch had instantly brought to life.

While she might not like him, she was wise enough to understand that it wasn't always about liking the other person. Sometimes it was about pure animal attraction.

Refusing to think about it, she turned to work. When she'd typed in the wrong figures three times, Gabby admitted she was too tired and too distracted. Time to call it a day.

As she was leaving, she spied Jon at his workbench in the shop. His head was propped on his hand as he studied blueprints. It wasn't until she got closer that she saw his eyes were shut.

He looked oddly boyish. There was something innocent and unguarded in his expression. She felt a weakening in her resistance to him.

"Jon." She put her hand on his shoulder, intending to shake him awake. Instead, it rested there like a caress.

His eyes snapped open.

"You were asleep."

"No, I was, uh, visualizing something on this design." He gestured to the blueprint in front of him then rubbed his eyes.

That gesture dealt a bigger blow to her resistance. She realized it wasn't only animal attraction pulling them together. She took a step backward as if to get away from the knowledge.

She cleared her throat. "I'm heading off now."

He gave her a smile, and she could see his exhaustion.

"Yeah, I should, too." He stood and stretched. The hem of his T-shirt rose as he arched his back and she caught a flash of hard male belly. She looked away, but it was too late. Her mind had committed the image to permanent memory.

And suddenly she knew, for good or bad, she'd never look at Jon the same way again.

Find out what happens next in ONE GOOD REASON, available August 2011 from Harlequin® Superromance®!

HSREXP0811

Celebrating

Blaze **10** *years of* red-hot reads

Featuring a special August author lineup of
six fan-favorite authors who have written
for Blaze™ from the beginning!

The Original Sexy Six:

Vicki Lewis Thompson
Tori Carrington
Kimberly Raye
Debbi Rawlins
Julie Leto
Jo Leigh

Pick up all six Blaze™
Special Collectors' Edition titles!

August 2011

USA TODAY *bestselling author*

Lynne Graham

introduces her new Epic Duet

THE VOLAKIS VOW

A marriage made of secrets...

Tally Spencer, an ordinary girl with no experience of
relationships... Sander Volakis, an impossibly rich and
handsome Greek entrepreneur. Sander is expecting to
love her and leave her, but for Tally this is love at first
sight. Little does he know that Tally is expecting his
baby...and blackmailing him to marry her!

PART ONE:
THE MARRIAGE BETRAYAL
Available August 2011

PART TWO:
BRIDE FOR REAL
Available September 2011

Available only from Harlequin Presents®.

Harlequin

SPECIAL EDITION

Life, Love, Family and Top Authors!

IN AUGUST, HARLEQUIN SPECIAL EDITION FEATURES
USA TODAY BESTSELLING AUTHORS
MARIE FERRARELLA AND *ALLISON LEIGH*.

THE BABY WORE A BADGE
BY *MARIE FERRARELLA*

The second title in the **Montana Mavericks:
The Texans Are Coming!** miniseries....

Suddenly single father Jake Castro has his hands full with
the baby he never expected—and with a beautiful young
woman too wise for her years.

COURTNEY'S BABY PLAN
BY *ALLISON LEIGH*

The third title in the **Return to the Double C** miniseries....

Tired of waiting for Mr. Right, nurse Courtney Clay takes
matters into her own hands to create the family she's
always wanted— but her surly patient may just be
the Mr. Right she's been searching for all along.

**Look for these titles and others in August 2011
from Harlequin Special Edition wherever books are sold.**

BIG SKY BRIDE, BE MINE! *(Northridge Nuptials)* by *VICTORIA PADE*
THE MOMMY MIRACLE by *LILIAN DARCY*
THE MOGUL'S MAYBE MARRIAGE by *MINDY KLASKY*
LIAM'S PERFECT WOMAN by *BETH KERY*

SEUSA0811